I0728072

THE TWELVE DEATHS OF CHRISTMAS

~ THE NOEL KRINGLE CHRONICLES ~

REBECCA M. SENESE

ALSO BY REBECCA M. SENESE

The Noel Kringle Chronicles (in reading order)

Santa Claus: Private Detective

Santa Must Die!

The Claus Connection

The Twelve Deaths of Christmas

Baby, It's Deadly Outside

Do You Fear What I Fear

The Man Who Would Be Santa

Who Killed Santa?

The Elf Who Saved Christmas

Wreck the Halls: 5 Christmas Horror Stories

A Very Zombie Christmas

The Santa Murders

THE TWELVE DEATHS OF CHRISTMAS

~ THE NOEL KRINGLE CHRONICLES ~

REBECCA M. SENESE

RFAR Publishing
Toronto, Canada

Printed and bound by IngramSpark.
Australia: Ingram Content Group AU Pty Ltd, Melbourne, Victoria.
US: Lightning Source LLC, La Vergne, Tennessee / Allentown, Pennsylvania / Jackson, Tennessee, United States.
UK: Lightning Source UK Ltd, Milton Keynes, United Kingdom.
Europe: Lightning Source UK Ltd, with facilities in Germany, France, and Spain.

Authorized Representative in the European Economic Area:
Lightning Source France
1 Av. Johannes Gutenberg, 78310
Maurepas, France.
compliance@lightningsource.fr

DEDICATION

For Donald E. Westlake

THE TWELVE DEATHS OF CHRISTMAS

~ THE NOEL KRINGLE CHRONICLES ~

CHAPTER

ONE

The snow outside wasn't terribly frightful but it was coming down steadily. Big fluffy flakes that drifted across the street as I walked. It had been snowing for the last hour or so, enough that a thin layer crunched under my boots.

Briefly, it reminded me of the North Pole, then a taxi zoomed by, spraying slush into the air. It seemed to hang for a moment before landing with a splat on my navy pea coat.

Before it could stain, I lifted my left hand and made a slight, flicking gesture. Nothing anyone around me would notice but it was enough to draw the snow off my coat. A moment later, the slush dropped to the sidewalk beside me.

Snow had never been a problem for me. I didn't have quite the control that I did when I lived at the North Pole but I still had enough magic to keep it off me.

I was Noel Kringle, youngest son of Kris Kringle, aka Santa Claus, hurrying to my latest job guarding the Toy Stash collected by the Bengali Foundation.

It was December 10th, the Toy Stash still had ten more days before Troy Bengali and his staff would gather them up and distribute them to needy families around Toronto. Ten more days for people to donate and, as a special commemoration for the foundation's tenth year running the Toy Stash, the Bengali Foundation was matching each donation.

As I walked along King Street toward the foundation's office near York, I wondered if any of the people around me were dropping off donations. Men and women hurried by, bundled in coats, scarves wrapped around their necks. Mittens and gloves clutched purses or plastic bags, handles of briefcases or large, paper shopping bags. The chill wind tugged at the wisps of hair poking out from under knit hats or around the edges of parka hoods.

Breath hung in the air like moist patches of fog. The air carried the crisp, cleanness of winter, even with the cars streaming by, belching exhaust.

Clouds crowded the sky above us, darkening the late afternoon to almost twilight. The sharp edges of the office towers softened in the snowfall. The granite and marble courtyards were hidden under rolls of snow.

Everything looked different and magical. My favourite time of year.

Of course.

Then I noticed a woman giving me an odd look as she

walked past. Casually, I glanced at a darkened window as I passed.

My wavy hair, usually brown, had started to turn white.

My beard, also usually brown and usually trimmed along my jaw line, was also whitening, and beginning to get bushy.

Damn the halls.

I had just dyed and trimmed both just over two weeks ago. I was going to have to do it again. And fast.

Like right now fast.

I glanced at my watch. My appointment at the Bengali Foundation was in fifteen minutes. I didn't have time to deal with my wayward hair and beard. I was going to have to take drastic action.

I pulled out my cell phone, an old flip phone since my magic interfered with smart phones, and opened it. I didn't bother to dial since the person I was calling didn't have a cell phone and wouldn't use it even if I gave it to him.

Fortunately he would hear me without it.

"Venir," I said. "I need your help. It's an emergency. Meet me in the drug store at Bay."

I closed the phone and tucked it into the pocket of my navy pea coat. Just a few more steps. I ducked my head. Trying to avoid looking at the people who were starting to take closer looks at me.

I really needed to get a hat. And it wasn't going to be a red one.

I hurried into the drug store just as one man lifted his

hand to point at me. He'd had the beginnings of a big smile on his face. He probably loved Christmas.

The aisles sped by as I almost ran down the length of the store. I skidded to a stop as I reached the hair dye aisle.

Halfway down stood my associate, Venir, an ex-Christmas Elf.

He was just over four feet tall and wore a boy's large khaki parka, unzipped, over a pair of jeans and a charcoal grey sweater. A dark green knit hat was perched on his head, hiding his large pointed ears. Wisps of his white hair curled around the edges of the hat.

His hands were stuffed into the pockets of the parka and I knew one of them would be clenching an unlit cigar. I never let him smoke in my office and there was no smoking in stores.

He did a double take when he saw me.

"Boss, your hair... your beard..."

"I know," I said. "You gotta help me with this fast."

He pulled his hands from his pocket. Sure enough the left one clutched the stump of an unlit cigar. He spread them in a helpless gesture.

"None of my magic is gonna work on you," he said. "You know that."

I sighed. I did know. The closer we got to Christmas, the more my hair and beard would take on the attributes of Santa Claus. I would never take over that job, my older brother KJ was in line when my dad retired, but my body didn't know that.

One of the challenges of being the youngest son of Kris Kringle. Not that I would have it any other way.

But the timing was damned inconvenient.

"You need to help me colour it," I said. I poked around the shelves until I found a spray-on dye. I pulled two cans down and handed them to Venir.

"Go pay for these and meet me in the alley two stores over," I said. "We'll have to work fast."

"Gotcha, boss. I'm on it."

He clutched the cans to his chest and hurried toward the cashier.

I headed back out onto the street.

It had darkened as the sun, hidden by the clouds, had gone down. Yellowish streetlights created dim shadows but it was enough for me to slip into the alley unnoticed.

I found an overhang half way down and stood under it, waiting for Venir. I brushed the few flakes of snow from my hair. When I rubbed my chin, I felt the length of my beard.

I should have told Venir to buy scissors too.

A moment later, the Elf appeared at the mouth of the alley. He moved toward me, carrying a white plastic bag. When he reached me, he pulled out a hand mirror.

"I thought you might need this too," he said.

"Great thinking," I said. "Let's do it."

He took one can and I took the other. I crouched down so he could reach me and we got to work.

I sprayed my beard while he worked on the back of my head. As I watched, the white hair disappeared under a misting of brown. The stench was acrid and chemical smelling, making my nostrils crinkle. Too much of this stuff and I'd be flying for my meeting.

Either that or I'd die from the chemical inhalations.

Before that happened, I finished colouring my beard and moustache. Through the mirror, I could see Venir starting on the left side of my head. So I got to work on my right.

The fumes made my eyes. I blinked rapidly and kept spraying. The bright, almost glowing, whiteness disappeared under a flat, bland brown. It didn't look at all natural but it was going to have to do, at least until I could get real dye and do a proper job.

One that I hoped managed to last as long as this one.

Sure, and dad would miss every other stocking this year.

It would never happen.

Venir finished before I did. A final few sprays and then I was done. I waved my can at him.

"Check to make sure we got everything," I said.

He poked all over my head. I heard the occasional spritz of spray. He lifted the hair over my right ear.

"You sprayed the top of your ear, boss," he said.

"Just leave it," I said. "Any place we missed?"

"Nope. Looks all brown ta me."

I handed him my can and stood up. My knees cracked. I shook out my legs to get the blood flowing again.

"I have to get to my meeting," I said. "Meet me back at the office after you pick up some more of the dye I like."

"What about what you got on?" he asked.

"This won't last long," I said. "I'll need to do the whole thing again sooner rather than later. Make sure you get the Benson Brown 312 that I like."

He nodded. The plastic bag crinkled in his hands as he shoved the mirror inside. I headed for the front of the alley. Snow crunched under my feet as I followed the tracks I had made walking in. When I reached the mouth of it, I turned.

"Thanks, Venir," I called back. "You really saved my butt."

The Elf looked up, surprised. For a brief moment, the melancholy look he'd been carting around for the last month vanished and a smile bloomed across his face.

I wanted to stick around and encourage more of that look but I was already late for my meeting. I gave him a wave and headed off.

The Bengali Foundation was another block away. In the darkness of late afternoon, the dark grey of the building looked almost black. The first two floors took up almost the entire block, then a thinner tower blossomed upward, stretching thirty storeys into the sky. In the darkness, I could only see the first ten or so storeys, the rest were lost to the clouds and the encroaching night.

A wave of heat blasted me as I pushed in through the double glass doors. I felt sweat spring from my forehead almost instantly as I hurried across the expanse of lobby and toward the bank of elevators on the left. A grey granite desk stretched between the two banks of elevators, manned by two security guards. One was watching something below the counter, probably the monitors. The second one smiled and pushed a clipboard across the counter surface in my direction.

"Can you sign in please, sir," he said. The tone of his voice insisting it wasn't a question.

I took the pen from his hand and scrawled my name and then tenth floor where I was meeting Troy Bengali. I hesitated when I got to the time slot.

"Can you tell me the time?" I asked.

The security guard, an older man of about fifty-five, reached into the breast pocket of his light grey shirt. I noticed the slim silver chain that ran out of the pocket and down beneath the counter. As he started to pull his hand out of the pocket I felt a tingling along my skin. My magic.

An image of a train flooded my mind. Black engine gleaming as it chugged around a circular track. A young boy sat in the centre, a blue and white conductor's hat perched on his head. He held a pocket watch in his hand that he checked from time to time, making sure the train ran on time. It was his favourite Christmas present ever.

"Sir," the loud voice broke into my thoughts. "I said it's almost six thirty."

I blinked. The security guard stood in front of me, a puzzled look crinkling his forehead and accenting the lines around his eyes. I could almost make out the boy in the man's face.

"Thanks," I said. I scrawled the time down and slid the pen back to him.

I pulled my hand away before he reached for it. I didn't want my magic to pick anything else up from him.

The bank of three elevators reflected back my newly brown hair and beard in brushed silver. I unbuttoned my coat and unwound the red scarf from my neck. The heat almost made me feel flushed.

I only had to wait a moment before the far elevator on the left dinged and the doors opened.

I stepped inside and was surrounded by mirrors.

Under the bright lights, I was able to get a good look at the slapdash job Venir and I had done. The flatness of the colour made my hair look muddy. My normal waves looked plastered down my skull. I tried to poke at them, tried to lift them up but my hair crunched in my hands.

I would blame it on the weather.

The elevator dinged on the tenth floor and the doors slid open. As I stepped out, I took one final glance in the mirror.

And noticed a thin line of brown dribbling down my left temple.

Damn the halls, the heat was making the hair dye run!

I dug in my pockets and found a crumpled napkin from my early morning bagel. I wiped the drip away. It didn't return.

For the moment.

This meeting was going to have to be as fast as humanly possible.

I headed down the hall toward Troy Bengali's office.

Plush grey carpet led the way. The walls were a rich

taupe sponged on and textured. Dark wood doors lined the hall. Silver name plates were inlaid into the wood spelling out names and positions, most of them vice president of something or other. At the end of the hall was a simple name plate reading Troy Bengali. No position listed. Not that he needed it to be when his family ran the foundation.

I knocked on the door when I reached it. A moment later, the door sprang open and Troy Bengali stood there.

He was a short man, maybe five foot two inches. He had olive skin and black, tightly curled hair cropped short on his squarish head. A thick black moustache spread above his upper lip but never managed to cover it. His brown eyes were so dark they were almost as black as his hair. He wore a well tailored navy suit with a dark grey tie. A smile spread across his mouth.

"Noel, come in, good to see you."

He stepped back and I entered his office. It stretched out before me. The same plush grey carpeting covered the floor. To my left was a seating area with a dark grey leather couch sitting along the wall. Two matching armchairs faced it across a dark, polished wood coffee table.

Just past that, a large wall unit took up the rest of the wall, filled with books, plaques, and certifications of the good work of the Bengali Foundation.

Sheer grey curtains covered the wall opposite where I stood and I knew they covered floor to ceiling windows that overlooked the lake to the south. But with the view lost to darkness, the curtains worked to reflect the light back into the room.

Troy's desk was to the right of the door. It was a large slab of glass on metal legs. A closed laptop sat in front of the dark grey, leather armchair. Two plain, grey chairs sat in front of his desk. That was where I had sat two weeks ago when Troy hired me to help guard his Toy Stash.

This time, Troy stretched a hand toward the seating area to the left. I followed his direction and sat down in one of the armchairs. The leather sank beneath me. I breathed in the rich scent. The leather on the arms were soft under my hands. I leaned back, enjoying the feel of it.

This was about as opposite of my office as I could get.

Troy sat down on the couch across from me. He stretched his arm across the back of the couch and crossed his ankle on his other knee.

"How are the donations going, Troy?" I asked.

"Fantastic," he said. "Just fantastic, Noel. People are really getting into the spirit of it this year. I couldn't be happier. And I have you to thank for it."

"Oh?" I said. "Why me?"

"That sign we put up under the donation sign, security by SC Private Investigations, Noel Kringle, President. It gives people the idea that Santa himself is watching over our toy drive and they want to get in on it. We're already almost double the donations from last year. It's just fantastic." He chuckled. "Of course, we have to match all those toys so it's going to be a stretch for our bottom line. But that's the kind of stretch I like making."

"Glad to hear it," I said. "So you're happy with Palle taking these shifts?"

"Oh yes, he's just great," Troy said. "He has a very regal bearing, and his size doesn't hurt either."

I smiled at Troy. He didn't know the half of it.

Palle Gudbrand, the newest addition to my private investigations firm, was a troll enchanted with a masking spell that made him look like a tall, burly man instead of his usual, light-green skinned, nine foot tall troll self, with huge tusks coming out from either side of his mouth and his pointed ears on either side of his bald head. He was still a troll under the masking spell and he could appear as a troll when he wanted to but while on a case, I insisted he keep the tall, burly man persona.

I nodded at Troy. "That's great."

"There's just one problem," he said.

I kept the smile on my face even as I felt my chest tighten. "Oh?"

"We're getting so many donations we can't keep them in our back lobby anymore." He chuckled. "What a problem to have. But we'll have to move them into the front lobby. There's enough space near the left wall for triple the size so I don't think we'll have any problem but it does mean I'll need more from you."

"What's that?" I asked.

"I want you to supervise the move of the Toy Stash, then

I'm going to need two staff with it during the daytime office hours. It's not that Palle isn't doing a great job it's just that the stash is getting so big."

"Of course I understand," I said. "Not a problem. I'll take care of it."

Troy grinned. "I knew you'd say that. So do you think you could move the stash tonight?"

I felt the smile frozen to my face. Move all those toys tonight?

I opened my mouth to suggestion something else but Troy gave a small hopeful smile. I could feel the tug that he wanted this most for Christmas.

What could I say?

"Okay," I said.

CHAPTER

TWO

I ducked away from Troy's profuse gushing thanks and headed to the back lobby on the main floor.

It was less than half the size of the front lobby of the building and the size was shrunken even more by the gigantic mound of toys sitting in the corner against the wall.

All manner of toys filled the space. Dolls, trucks, cars, bats, board games, and more piled higher than my head.

"Noel, you are much too early to be relieving me," a deep voice sounded behind me.

I turned.

Palle Gudbrand stood behind me. He had dropped the mask and I saw his troll self. Lights from the pocked ceiling lights glinted on the green skin of his scalp. His ears almost curled up over his head, reminding me of Venir's. The huge tusks in his mouth gave Palle's smile a threatening look if you didn't know him as I did.

I had met Palle when he had been under the influence of a spirit who had tempted him from the Magical Realms. Using Palle, the spirit had invaded people's bodies and souls, burning through them, leaving husks of charred stone-like bodies behind as it looked for one that could contain it. I had managed to stop the spirit and cast it down into the Under-well, the magical prison where all the entities who broke the bounds and laws of the realms were locked away.

Upon regaining his freedom, Palle had decided that he owed me and was going to stick around until he repaid me for saving him. Never mind that he had saved my older brother KJ, Palle still thought he owed me.

So I was trying to find ways for him to pay me back so he could go home.

"I'm not here to relieve you, Palle," I said. "Troy has asked that we move the Toy Stash to the front lobby as it's getting too big for the back lobby. He's then asked for two people to guard it during the day."

Palle frowned. "I am able to guard it myself."

"I know that," I said. "But no one else can see how big you really are. Remember, they just think you're a burly guy over six feet tall, not a troll almost nine feet tall."

"Of course," he said. "When are we to move the pile?"

"Now," I said. "I'll show you where they're to go."

I led him past the elevators and pointed at the walls near the windows. He nodded.

"I can do that easily."

He turned away and headed back past the elevators. His heavy steps reverberated through the granite floor. I glanced over at the security guards. Neither looked up. Palle's mask must have held.

I followed Palle but he was already heading back toward me. He held a pile of toys in his arms so high they almost towered over his head. I darted out of the way as he came lumbering forward. With a bent knee, he gently placed the pile down on the floor, then headed back to gather another pile.

To my surprise, Palle managed to carry all the toys in three trips. Finally, he retrieved the Bengali Foundation Toy Stash sign with the notation about SC Private Investigations underneath. He set the metal base of the sign in front of the pile and stepped back.

"Does it look all right?" he asked.

"Looks great," I said. "You didn't have to do it all yourself."

He glanced at me and smiled. He was far too polite to make a note of how useless I would have been compared to him.

"Venir and I will relieve you in the morning around eight," I said.

"That is sooner than you are scheduled," he said.

"Yes, but we'll cover the daytime shift together. You can get some rest and come back tomorrow evening around six."

"I could easily stay through the day," he said. "I don't need as much rest as you."

I stepped closer and turned my back so the security guards wouldn't hear me.

"I know, Palle, but you have to act as close to human as possible. No one knows you're a troll. They won't understand how you have the stamina to stay on guard for days at a time."

He chewed his upper lip, looking thoughtful. The whiteness of his tusks glinted in the light. Finally he nodded.

"Okay, Noel," he said.

I patted his arm. His bicep was almost thicker than my head.

"Have a good night," I said. "I'll see you in the morning."

"Good night, Noel."

I headed out into the cold, grateful that my hair hadn't dripped any more.

The street was emptier now. The crowds heading out for end of day shopping or just heading home had dispersed. The occasional car drove along the street, tires hissing against the wet pavement. A red streetcar clanged its bell as it passed me. The lit up interior showed it half full of people hunched against the cold.

I breathed in the crisp evening air. I could feel the temperature dropping. The snow had stopped falling, leaving a fresh layer of clean white over the sidewalk. It was at times like this that Toronto reminded me most of the North Pole.

I returned to the alley where Venir and I had covered the white that had sprang up on my hair and beard. Even though the traffic was light, I didn't want any witnesses to what I was about to do. I made sure I retreated far enough into the alley to be invisible from the road.

Then I would *wink* back to the office.

A *wink* was one of the few magical things I could still do in Toronto, as long as I limited myself. In the space of a wink, I could transport myself from one place to another. With Venir's training, I had learned to anchor several locations around the city in my mind. This allowed me to use less magic to get there, giving me more opportunities to use my limited magical reserves.

As an ex-Christmas Elf, Venir didn't have my limitations, but my magic was undeniably linked to the North Pole. Living away from the North Pole meant giving up much of my magic. It was the price I had to pay to be a private detective in Toronto.

I heard the telltale hiss of another car approaching. I waited until it passed the opening of the alley.

Then I *winked*.

I landed in my battered, leather chair behind my metal desk that I had bought secondhand at Goodwill. My own laptop sat on the left side of my desk. Two hardback, wooden chairs butted almost to the front of my desk. There was enough space for me to slip around the right side of my desk and in three paces, I would be at the door that led to my waiting area.

Just outside the door, along the right wall, sagged a brown leather couch. The leather was dull and scuffed looking. Three yellow plastic chairs huddled against the far wall to the left of the door leading out to the hallway.

To my left was the small half bath, with a toilet and a sink. Just over two weeks ago, I had been bent over that sink, rinsing out brown hair dye.

I had always liked this office but somehow compared to Troy Bengali's it was looking a little rough.

I shook my head. Stop comparing. We had different lives. Different priorities.

My priority was to make sure I had enough hair dye to get me through the season.

"Venir," I called into the air.

A moment later, he appeared before me, hands holding two plastic bags.

"I tried, boss, but they didn't have that brand number," he said. "The clerk said they stopped makin' it. So I got you some of these. Thought you could see if they work."

He held up the bags.

"What do you mean they stopped making it," I said. "They can't stop making it. It's just a brown colour."

Venir shook his head. "That was Brown 312. A more carmelly shade. They replaced it with Brown 714 but it's more... browny. Here, look."

He pulled out a box and held it out to me. I took it. The colour looked ashen, not the warm, caramel brown that I needed.

I set the box on one of the plastic chairs and took the bag from him. Inside, each box was a slightly different shade of brown, chocolatey, ash, dark, light, muddy, warm. I'd had no idea brown hair colour came in so many shades.

And none of them quite as close as the now discontinued 312.

I picked out one that was a slightly darker colour. Maybe being darker meant it would last a little longer.

Sure. And the temperature would jump fifty degrees tomorrow.

I held up the box.

"Let's do this one," I said. "I'll just add it right over top this spray-on stuff."

Venir nodded. "Good choice, kiddo. Especially doin' it now."

Oh no. I pushed past him and headed for the bathroom. I hit the switch and the single bulb snapped on. I stared at myself in the mirror above the sink.

White patches were already starting to show in my hair and my beard.

I sighed. At least the spray-on had lasted long enough for the meeting. I cracked open the box.

"Could you give me a hand, Venir?" I asked.

BY THE TIME WE RELIEVED PALLE THE NEXT MORNING, THE BROWN in my hair and beard had settled in. The box dye had a little more richness to it, looking more natural than the spray-on stuff. Good thing, especially in the crisp morning sunshine.

The day was bright and clear. Cold chilled the air, making everyone's breath into puffs that looked like smoke. I remembered pretending to be a fire-breathing dragon as a kid just because the cold air of the North Pole made breathing produce those smoke-like clouds from my breath. Now everyone on the street looked the same.

The sidewalks were mostly clear but my boots still crunched on the ice particles left over on the pavement. I wore my navy pea coat and red scarf over black dress pants and a dark blue shirt. Venir stood beside me wearing his parka. I'd encouraged him to ditch the jeans so he wore black pants similar to mine and a lime green pull over.

No one would miss him in that.

The Bengali Foundation building looked grander in the morning light. The grey granite seemed to sparkle and glitter in the light. The tower rose upward like a powerful sentinel in the clear, blue sky.

Venir followed me as I pushed through the front double glass doors. The lobby was busy with people dressed in suits and long coats, hurrying to the elevators. A single security guard sat at the desk in between the two banks. He was new and had probably just started his day shift.

Just like Venir and I were about to do.

To the left, the toy pile managed to look large and imposing but also smaller than last night. There was still lots of space in the lobby, like Troy had mentioned. Lots more room for the pile to grow and I hoped it would over the next nine days.

To the right of the pile near the wall stood Palle. He stood upright, arms behind his back, his feet about shoulders-width apart. He looked alert and fresher than I felt. In his human persona, he had brown hair cut close to the scalp and the beginnings of stubble darkened his cheeks.

Venir and I crossed to him.

"How was your night, Palle?" I asked.

"It was uneventful," he said. "Peaceful and quiet."

"So no problems? Any questions from the security guards?"

He shook his head. "Nothing. Mr. Troy left shortly after midnight. Nothing happened after that."

"Great, we'll take over now," I said. "You get some rest and be back for six."

A flicker of a frown crossed Palle's human face. "Noel, I do not need to rest. I could easily stay here today."

I leaned closer, aware of the steady stream of people walking past us just a few feet away.

"Palle, we talked about this last night. I don't want to raise any suspicions."

"Yeah, c'mon Palle," Venir said. "Give us a chance to watch folks dropping off donations."

Now the frown deepened on Palle's face. "You always see

the donations being dropped off. No one drops off any during the night."

Now we were getting to the issue. Palle wanted to be around for the toy drop-offs.

"How about this," I said. "You take off today and tomorrow I'll let you stay all day."

Palle's frown faded. He gave a satisfied nod. "Okay."

"Great. See you at six."

"Good day, Noel. Venir."

The troll gave us a bow of his head then, picking up his coat from the floor behind him, he headed for the front doors.

I watched until he reached the sidewalk, tugging on his puffy winter coat and heading east.

"Okay, Venir," I said. "Let's get set up."

For the day shift, security let us stash our coats in their staff room, just off the second bank of elevators. I took Venir's coat with me and hung them both up in the closet of the staff room. It was a long, narrow room with a fake wood veneer table running down the centre. Folding chairs were tucked along the length of it. A coffee maker burbled away in the corner, filling the room with the rich smell of fresh coffee.

I snagged two cups in grey Bengali Foundation mugs and carried them out to the front. I handed one to Venir and crossed to the security desk to deliver the second mug.

The security guard, a young man in his twenties, looked up surprised as I set the mug on the counter.

"I thought you might like a fresh cup," I said. "I'm Noel Kringle doing security for the Toy Stash." I jerked at thumb at the mound of toys behind me.

"Right," the security guard said. "I heard about that. I'm just back from vacation. This is usual shift. I'm Eric Laytham."

"Nice to meet you, Eric," I said.

He took the mug and blew on the surface of the coffee.

"If you guys need to take a break or somethin', I'll be happy to watch the toys," he said.

I smiled. "Thanks for the offer but there's two of us during the day now. We'll be fine."

He gave me a nod and I headed back toward Venir. The Elf was already sipping away at the coffee. He gave me a thumbs up.

"I'm going to get myself a cup," I said. He nodded, taking another sip.

I headed back into the staff room. The coffee pot was just about empty so I set another pot to percolate. While I waited, listening to the cheerful gurgle of the coffee maker, I glanced at the large bulletin board that lined the left side of the wall. Duty schedules for the security and maintenance staff were tacked onto the left side. On the right were notices of events happening in and around the building. In the centre were copies of news clippings about the foundation. Tacked right on top was the announcement about the tenth year of the Toy Stash.

A photo of the smiling Troy Bengali standing in front of

the granite steps of the building filled the top of the story. It had obviously been taken in the summer. Troy wore only his suit and there wasn't even a hint of snow. Even still in the photograph, Troy's boisterous personality came through. It looked like he had been snapped in between bouncing on his heels or a quick dash to follow up on something.

Beside me, the coffee machine gave a final loud burble as it spat out the last of the coffee. I listened to it dribbling away into the pot.

Instead of grabbing a cup, I stepped closer to the bulletin board to read the story about the Toy Stash. It started with a brief history of the Bengali Foundation, how it was founded by Troy's great grandfather and how Troy's father started the Toy Stash two years before retiring. Since then, Troy had built up the Toy Stash so that it had grown to support almost two hundred families. This year looked to top even that amount.

The article folded under at the point. I reached up to unpin it so I could read the rest.

A smeared line from a red marker covered the rest of the article. Written in block letters above the line was the word LIAR.

Someone wasn't such a fan of Troy Bengali. Interesting.

I folded the paper back up and pinned it back into place. I wondered if I should mention it to Troy but what would be the point? Not everyone liked their job or the company they worked for. It would only upset Troy.

I turned to the coffee maker and poured myself a cup of coffee.

The morning passed quickly. Several people arrived to drop off donations. We made note of each one on the donation sheet and had folks initial. Several people asked to take photos of the Toy Stash, some with themselves posed in front, others asked to include us in the photos too. More than once we had to ask Eric the security guard to take the photo.

Everyone left smiling and happy and the Toy Stash continued to grow. I was starting to see why Palle had wanted to stick around. I would figure out a way to let him have every other day shift, that way he could enjoy seeing people donate.

It even seemed to cheer Venir.

I had noticed since early November Venir had been gruffer than usual. I tried to talk to him about it but he always changed the subject or had to suddenly be somewhere else. I knew it might be difficult for him to talk to me about whatever was bothering him, I was his boss after all, but I hoped I was also his friend. Still he hadn't felt comfortable enough to talk to me about it. I only hoped that he would feel that way eventually.

It was only after lunch, when I'd taken a few minutes to run to the deli down the street that I realized I hadn't see Troy all morning.

As I carried back a ham and cheese for myself and a tuna on rye for Venir, I thought about it. Troy usually popped down from his office once in the morning and once in the middle of the afternoon. Maybe work had kept him busy this morning but it nagged at me. Troy had never let his busy schedule keep him away before and now that the Toy Stash had been moved to the front lobby, I would have thought he would have liked to look in on it.

Back in the lobby, I handed Venir the sandwiches. He headed for the staff room to eat out of sight. When he was finished, I would go in and have mine.

While I waited, I wandered over to the security desk, still keeping an eye on the Toy Stash. I leaned on the granite counter, feeling the cool, hard surface through the fabric of my shirt.

"Eric, can you tell me what time Troy Bengali came in this morning?" I asked.

"Sure, Noel," Eric said. I heard the tapping of his fingers on the keys. Then a soft hrmph.

"That's strange," he said.

I glanced over at him, noting the frown on his face, and then looked back at the toy mound.

"What's strange?" I asked.

"Mr. Bengali hasn't signed in yet," he said.

"Are you sure?" I asked. "He didn't mention anything about not being in today, did he?"

"He didn't say. Usually he lets us know here. He's real thoughtful that way." More tapping sounded. "Nope, he didn't sign in at all."

He continued tapping away while I stared at the mound of toys. An queasy feeling was starting in the pit of my stomach and it wasn't from hunger. In fact, I don't think I'd ever felt less hungry.

"Now this really is odd," Eric said.

"What is?" I asked. My mouth felt dry and almost sour.

"According to the sign outs from last night, Mr. Troy didn't sign out."

"Could there have been a mistake?" I asked. "Maybe he left without signing out."

"Mr. Troy would never do that," Eric said. "He takes building security very seriously. He always says that. He always says we're the front lines in protecting the tenants of the building. He's a stickler for getting folks signed in and out."

The queasy feeling in my stomach deepened into outright nausea. Something bad had happened. I was sure of it.

I had never wanted to be wrong more in my life.

"Maybe he's still here," I said. Even saying it sounded ridiculous. It was almost twelve thirty. Even a workaholic like Troy Bengali needed sleep.

"I'll call up to his office." Eric lifted the telephone receiver. I heard him murmuring into it. I kept watch on the Toy Stash.

It reached almost halfway up the wall. The bottom spread out like a puddle, with a few wayward toys on the floor aways from the bottom edge. Venir and I would neaten up the edge after lunch. I could see a few dolls, a truck, a wayward Monopoly game, a foot.

Um. What?

That couldn't be right.

Eric continued murmuring behind me as I took a few steps toward the Toy Stash. For a brief moment, the Monopoly box blocked the view of the foot, then as I took another step closer, the foot appeared again. It was clad in a black, leather shoe. Black laces were neatly tied on the top. The design carved into the leather was delicate, intricate, subtle. A rich design. Italian, or so I had been told.

Told by Troy Bengali.

I stopped at the edge of the Toy Stash and reached down. I moved several dolls and a chemistry set, enough to confirm that the foot in the shoe was attached to a leg, dressed in a familiar dark grey suit.

I turned back to Eric, just as he hung up the phone.

"Mr. Troy isn't upstairs," he said. His voice carried across the expanse of the lobby.

I waited until a final lone man in a taupe overcoat hurried into the elevator, leaving the lobby empty except for Troy and me.

"I know," I called over to the young security guard. "Troy didn't leave the building. You'd better call the police."

THREE

Detective Lieutenant Stan Mallory frowned at me as he stood at the base of the Toy Stash. Several panel barriers had been erected, hiding the Toy Stash from view of the exterior windows.

Compared to the elegant décor around him, Stan Mallory was a crumpled mess. His black suit looked almost like he'd slept in it. The crease in his pants was off centre and veered to the side. Wrinkles lined his white shirt. Even his dark taupe winter coat had crease marks.

"Noel," he said. "Why are you always standing over bodies?"

"I'm not *always* standing over bodies," I said. I tried not to sound petulant. From the sour look on Mallory's face, I didn't quite succeed.

I had met Mallory on my first case in Toronto, in somewhat similar circumstances. I had been arrested standing over a body and had only convinced Mallory I hadn't killed the man by revealing who I really was. It had taken some convincing, namely knowing his favourite Christmas present was a somewhat battered Mattel police car with an unfortunate tendency to list to the left and then producing said car. When that hadn't quite convinced him all the way, helping me to defeat a goblin bent on destruction had finished the job.

We had developed a somewhat begrudging friendship held together by occasional assistance and copious amounts of Gellers scotch, a magical blend brewed by Gnomes.

Except I wasn't too thrilled about the look I was getting from him.

"You're definitely standing over this one," Mallory said. He nodded at the Toy Stash.

Three police officers in uniform stood around the base of the mound of toys near the wall. They had excavated into the toy mound, uncovering the rest of what had been revealed to be the dead body of Troy Bengali.

Troy lay on a bed of toys, his limbs spread out as if he'd been a rag doll tossed on the pile. His head hung at an odd angle, indicating he had probably died of a broken neck.

"What's it look like, Horace?" Mallory said to one of the officers. The officer, a black man with black hair silvered with grey cut close to his head, gestured at the body with one latex gloved hand.

"Lividity looks like he's been dead several hours. I'd say

death occurred sometime in the middle of the night. The coroner would know better."

Mallory nodded. He glanced over at me.

"How long have you been here?" he asked.

The sour tension in my stomach tightened. "Since eight in the morning."

Mallory waved at the Toy Stash sign and the notification of SC Private Investigations providing security. "You have someone on guard duty overnight?"

I swallowed around a lump in my throat. "Yes."

Mallory pursed his lips. "You gonna make me ask, Noel?"

I didn't want to say it because I knew it couldn't be true. But I had to answer. Mallory wouldn't take my opinion for it.

"Palle was on duty last night," I said. "He didn't mention anything out of the ordinary."

Mallory nodded. "You know where we can find Palle?"

"I'll bring him in," I said.

"Noel..."

"Stan, please," I said. "I'll bring him in, I promise."

Mallory huffed out a breath. He waved at the black officer. "Horace Latimer will go with you. Sorry, Noel. There's a procedure that has to be followed. I know you won't try to coach him..."

He let the words trail off with a shrug of his shoulders.

Sure, he knew I wouldn't coach Palle but he couldn't take the chance.

I nodded. "Okay. Let me talk to Venir first."

I ducked around the closest panel. Venir stood beside the

security desk. His arms were crossed over his chest. As soon as I appeared, he released his arms and took a step forward.

"What's happening?" he asked.

I tilted my head toward the front door. Venir followed. As we stopped in front of the glass panel, I noticed Officer Latimer step out from behind the barrier. He watched us but didn't move forward.

I turned back to Venir.

"Troy Bengali is dead," I said. "He died sometime last night and somehow ended up buried under the Toy Stash."

Venir frowned. "Last night? How could that happen last night? Palle woulda seen 'em."

"He should have," I agreed. "The police want to talk to him."

Venir tilted his head. "Why? He woulda said somethin' to you." He stopped and his face paled as realization struck him. "They don't think... not Palle."

"I agree," I said. "I can't imagine he did it but they want to talk to him now. We can't delay it." I gestured at Officer Latimer.

"The officer and I will go get Palle," I said. "I need you to find out what kind of magic can fool a troll."

"Magic? You think it was magic?"

"What else could it be?" I said. "Palle would have seen anything else."

"Yeah, you're right," he said. "I'll look into it."

I nodded and stepped back. When Officer Latimer saw me move, he started toward me. I waited by the door and together we pushed through the double glass doors into the cold, bright day.

PALLE LIVED IN A RUNDOWN LOFT IN THE EAST END OF TOWN. IT was one room that barely seemed large enough for a troll but with twelve foot high ceilings, it had one very attractive quality for him.

The fresh, white snow had turned to slush by the time we reached the end of his street. The old warehouse where Palle lived seemed to hunch under the bright, blue sky. The red brick looked dull and leeched of colour. Mounds of snow covered the roof, deep enough that I couldn't tell if it was arched or flat. The walkway from the sidewalk was still clogged with slush and snow. Office Latimer and I kicked our way through it.

At the front door, an old style intercom system in cracked, beige plastic was tacked onto the wall beside the front door. I pressed the button for Palle's apartment and listened to the tiny buzz through the small speaker. After a moment, I heard a click and then Palle's rich tones sounded, still sounding warm through the cheap speaker.

"Hello," he said.

"Palle, it's Noel," I said. "Can you let me in, I need to talk to you."

"Should you not be guarding the Toy Stash, Noel?" Palle's voice sounded concerned.

"It's fine for the moment," I said. "I really need to speak with you."

"Very well. Come in."

A buzz sounded followed by a loud click. I grabbed the door before it finished and pulled it open. Officer Latimer caught the edge and held the door open for me.

"After you," he said. I thought I heard sympathy in his voice but I couldn't be sure.

I stepped past him and through the front door. The interior hallway was a flat white like unpainted drywall. The tile started as off white, speckled with black and blue flecks then changed to a black and white tile part way down the hall. The doors were faded wood and looked thin enough to kick through.

Palle lived at the back. Even before I reached his door, I heard the click of the lock and a creak as the door opened. He poked his head out. For a brief moment, I caught a glimpse of light-green skin and light glinting of the edge of a tusk, then the mask of his human persona dropped down. As a human, he had a wide nose and thin lips. He looked perplexed to see the police officer behind me.

"Is there a problem?" he asked as I reached the door.

I took a breath and let it out. This was the part I wasn't looking forward to.

"There was an... incident at the Bengali Foundation," I said. "Last night."

Concern rippled over Palle's face. Again, I almost caught a glimpse of the troll beneath. Emotion seemed to weaken his control.

"What incident?" he said.

"Troy Bengali is dead," I said. "We found him this morning. Under the Toy Stash."

Palle frowned. "That can't be right. I was there the entire time. I didn't see him or anyone else, other than the security guards."

Officer Latimer stepped up to stand beside me.

"Were you awake the entire time, sir?" he said. His tone was gentle. "Maybe you took a break, just for a few minutes. Went into the staff room for some coffee."

Relief almost made me feel weak. Latimer was trying to help Palle, see if there was any way out for him, but Palle didn't take it.

He shook his head. "No, I didn't take any breaks. I was awake the entire time."

"In that case, please step out here, sir." Office Latimer stepped back, making room for Palle.

I wanted to tell Palle not to come out of his home. Close the door and call a lawyer but one glance told me Latimer were arrest me for obstruction if I did anything to dissuade Palle.

I felt helpless. Palle didn't know what was happening and I couldn't warn him.

He shrugged and stepped out into the hallway beside me.

In one smooth movement, Officer Latimer slipped

behind him and grabbed one of Palle's arms. The metal of the handcuffs clicked as he snapped it onto Palle's wrist.

"I'm sorry, sir, but you're under arrest. Please come quietly back to the station with me."

Bewilderment flooded Palle's face. His mouth gapped open.

"Noel?" he said.

"Go with him," I said. "It'll be all right. I'll get a lawyer and we'll take care of this. I promise, Palle. I know you didn't do anything."

"Didn't do anything," he repeated. Slowly, awareness dawned on his face. His eyes widened. "You think I killed Mr. Bengali?"

"I don't," I said.

Palle started to twist. His arm snapped out of Latimer's grip. Palle looked back over his shoulder at the officer.

"You think I did it!"

Latimer's voice remained calm. "I'm just doing my job, sir. They just need to ask you questions about what happened last night."

"Why do you need these things on me to ask questions?"

I could hear the anger warring with the confusion in Palle's voice. Any minute now he would forget about having only human strength. He would be able to snap those hand-cuffs apart like taffy.

Then the whole persona would drop.

I could *not* let him reveal his troll self.

I grabbed Palle's upper arm and squeezed. His head swung around toward me. His eyes looked glazed.

"Palle, trust me. I will look after this." I focused on him, seeing all his favourite presents from the Claus Sante Troll, another of dad's identities when he crossed over into the Magical Realms.

After a moment, Palle's eyes cleared. I could see him looking at me, see the confusion and anger warring inside, both of them hiding something I didn't realize was there.

Fear.

Palle was afraid.

I gave his shoulder another squeeze. "It's going to be okay, Palle. I promise."

The rock hard muscle under my palm relaxed, turning from a hardness of granite back into softer flesh. He bowed his head.

"Okay."

"He'll be at the station," Latimer said. "I'll walk him through booking myself."

"Thanks," I said.

Without another word, Latimer took Palle's arm and began steering him back down the way we'd come.

The last I saw of Palle was his glance over his shoulder as they turned to exit the front door. His lips moved and I swear I saw a hint of tusk at the corner of his mouth as he mouthed the words 'help me'.

Then the front door clicked shut behind them and I was left alone with my helplessness.

CHAPTER

FOUR

I headed back to my office, intending to find a lawyer for Palle. I didn't really know any lawyers and the only people I could think of to contact to ask for advice were no longer available or appropriate. I didn't think Mallory would be able to help.

And unfortunately Troy Bengali was no longer available to help.

I sank into my faded leather chair and opened my laptop. As it powered up, I pulled the office phone closer so I'd be able to dial when I found someone that might work out.

Then a faint whiff of ginger bread filled the air.

Even before the computer finished booting up my brother Kris Junior appeared. He wore a pair of jeans stuffed into black boots with a white puffed edge. Gone was his usual red flannel shirt, replaced with a more traditional red.

His hair was pure white, slicked back in waves from his forehead and his beard was bushier than usual, extending almost halfway to his chest.

He looked more like dad than ever.

He flopped down into the closest hard back chair and swung his boots up onto my desk.

"Noel, you are lucky you got out when you could," he said.

"KJ, I've got a bit of a situation here," I said. "What do you want?"

He swung his boots off the desk and leaned forward. He jabbed a finger at me.

"Hey, what have you got to bitch about?" he said. "I'm up to my eyes with cranky Elves, trying to keep the triple shifts going without anybody burning out. I've two reindeer out with the bird flu. The sleigh needs new runners and they're backordered. And we're still getting in wishes from late requestors."

I closed my eyes and counted to ten. I had to remember when I needed someone to fill in for me as a Santa for a Christmas in July event, KJ had come through and that he had actually shown some appreciation for my job.

Once.

When I decided that I wasn't going to leap across the desk and strangle him, I opened my eyes.

"I'm sorry it's tense for you, KJ," I said. "But like I said, I've got a bit of a situation. The man I was working for is dead and the police have arrested Palle on suspicion."

The annoyed look faded from KJ's face. "Palle. That's the troll, isn't it?"

"Yes."

"What happened to your boss?" he asked.

"He wasn't my boss, he was my client," I said. "Sometime last night someone killed him and buried him under the Toy Stash."

"Toy stash? What's that?"

"It's a toy collection sponsored by the Bengali Foundation. They collect toys until December 20th and then distribute them to needy families. This year was their tenth year and the foundation was going to match every toy donation. Troy Bengali was running it and he hired me to provide security."

"Do you know how he was killed?" KJ asked.

I shook my head. "Not yet. Mallory hadn't even called the coroner yet."

"Maybe it was natural causes," KJ said.

I blinked at him and tilted my head.

KJ shrugged. "You never know."

"So he decided to bury himself under the mound of toys right before he died," I said. "Right under Palle's nose and did it so well that Palle didn't even notice."

"Hey, I said it was a possibility not that it actually *happened.*"

I shook my head. Sometimes it appeared that KJ understood how the world worked, but then comments like that indicated the boundaries of his understanding.

"Trust me, it's not a possibility," I said.

"So what are you going to do?" he said.

"First I have to find a lawyer for Palle," I said, "and I've got Venir out looking for ways a troll could be fooled."

At the mention of Venir's name, KJ grimaced for a moment. The effect was so short if he hadn't done at other times I would have discounted it. But he did it every time I mentioned Venir. There was a story there, something that had caused Venir to leave the North Pole behind and earned KJ's distain. One of these days I'd get it out of one of them.

"A lawyer," KJ said. "Why don't you use one of dad's?"

"Um, dad has lawyers?"

"Of course, there's always some idiot trying to sue because the present is wrong or Santa doesn't exist or something nonsense. He's got them all over the world." KJ shook his head. "You never did pay any attention to the business aspect of it all."

I shrugged. Being second in line, I knew I would never have to take over so why pay attention to the minutia?

Maybe because it might be helpful for *my* business.

"So does dad have any lawyers here in Toronto?" I asked.

"Only the best firm in the city," KJ said. "Rutherford, Henderson, Judges, and Sloan."

The name ran a bell. I think I'd read articles online in the Toronto news site about them. They defended high profile clients.

Palle wasn't high profile, but Troy Bengali certainly was.

Had been.

That along with dad's name might just get me in the door.

"Do you think you can recommend me?" I asked.

KJ sighed. He leaned back in the chair and lifted his boots up onto my desk. He knew I hated that and I knew I'd have to let him if I wanted any help out of him.

"Well, let me see," he said. "I could put in a good word. You are my brother, after all. But I'm awfully busy right now. I don't know when I'd find the time."

He'd found the time to come visit me for the purpose of complaining. But it might not be a good idea to mention that.

"Now if you were to do me a favour," he said.

Here it was. The real reason for his visit. Complaining hadn't been the reason after all. Or if it had been, it wasn't the only one.

"What favour?" I asked.

"Remember I mentioned the sleigh needs new runners," he said. "Dad told me to order them in August. Well, I got all caught up in that Claus Connection thing. I didn't get a chance to. Then we got so busy and well..."

"You forgot," I said. "When did you place the order?"

"Two days ago," he said.

"Two days!"

"All you have to do is follow up and then if they don't get them in stock by the end of the week..."

I sighed. I knew it was coming.

"If they don't get them in stock, what?"

"Find another set of runners."

"KJ, you know those runners are specially made. It's already December 10th."

"I would look for them myself," he said. "But I've got all these other things to do, as well as write that recommendation letter."

I pressed my lips tight together to stop myself from yelling at him. Palle was in trouble. I had to keep thinking about that, not about my brother's petty power play.

"Fine," I said. "I'll find the runners. But you'd better guarantee one of those lawyers for Palle and they'd better get him out of jail fast."

"Don't worry about it," KJ said. "They'll get him out first thing in the morning."

"The morning!"

"If not sooner."

I wagged my finger at him. "They'd better. And you'd better get on it now."

He held up his hands. "Consider it done, Noel. What's a big brother for."

Before I could give him a list, he vanished, leaving behind a slight lingering scent of ginger bread.

Then I noticed my special notebook, a gift from my mother, had flipped open to a page in the middle of the book. In KJ's scrawl was the name and phone number for the company he'd tried to order the sleigh runners from.

I sighed and picked up the phone. Maybe I'd get lucky and they'd have KJ's order in stock.

Naturally they didn't but they were nice enough to confirm that the earliest they'd be able to get a set of those specially made runners was January 16th, as they'd quoted the gentleman who had placed the order just the other day.

He'd known, and he'd come here specifically to foist it off on me. That way if I screwed it up he could still be the golden son in my father's eyes while it was fortunate I was the second son since I couldn't even be trusted to get the proper sleigh runners on time.

I resisted the urge to throw the phone across my office. Instead, I went online to see if I could find another company or two to check out.

But first I was going to see if KJ had at least kept his promise.

I checked my email and found a message from a Nadia Judges from Rutherford, Henderson, Judges, and Sloan. She was confirming her participation in the case and that she would be applying for bail immediately as well as a review of the arrest warrant. She concluded with her assurance that she believed the charges were baseless and would be thrown out of court before the week was up.

If she managed that, I was more than happy to find a set of runners for dad's sleigh.

Then I was going to find out who had killed Troy Bengali.

As usual, my Internet searching skills proved not up to the task of finding a competent supplier of runners for sleighs. The list started with three on point but soon devolved into lists for running shoes and other nonsensical entries.

There was only one option for me. I picked up the phone and called Shirl.

Shirl Trombley had become my defacto computer expert and charged accordingly. In fact, I had expected her rates to soar after I talked her into joining the Claus Connection, an online dating site for people who loved Christmas. It had been part of a missing person's case which had stretched to include stone bodies and ended with Shirl being one of the people disappeared by the spirit as a potential host. When I had vanquished it to the Under-well, I had saved her life.

So her rates didn't go up. Unfortunately, they didn't really go down either.

Shirl picked up on the first ring. "Talk."

"Shirl, it's Noel. I need to find a company that makes a special kind of runner for my dad's sleigh."

She paused on the other end. I heard a click of tapping on a keyboard.

"You got specs for 'em?" she asked.

"I can get them."

"Send them to me. I'll look around. When you need 'em by?"

"As soon as possible," I said. "Price is no object."

"Oh really?" she said. "I'm still waitin' for payment on my last invoice."

"I didn't say I was paying for it," I said. "My brother will be. And I'll get your payment by the end of next week."

"Promise?"

"I'll do my best," I said.

She hrmphed in my ear. "Send me the specs."

"Will do."

She hung up before I finished speaking. I let the receiver fall from my fingers and clatter down into place on the phone. I really had intended to pay her with funds from my next cheque.

Unfortunately, with Troy Bengali dead, I didn't know if I'd be getting paid or not. Probably not.

Maybe I'd tack on a finder's fee to that sleigh runner order. At least then I could pay Shirl for her time even if my month would be lean.

I copied down the specs for the runners and emailed them to Shirl. I knew them by heart. It was kind of hard to grow up at the North Pole and not absorb some things.

After I sent it, I opened my mouth to call for Venir when my phone rang. Had Shirl found someone already? I'd only just sent off the specs. She was a computer and Internet wiz but she couldn't possibly have found someone for me so quickly.

I picked up the phone. "Hello?"

"Noel, what are you playin' at?" Mallory's voice growled low through the ear piece.

"What do you mean, Stan?"

"You send some high fallutin' lawyer down here yelling about police harassment and you don't even bother to give me a heads up. I thought we were friends."

Uh oh. I hadn't realized this Judges woman would work so fast and cause such a problem. She was just supposed to get Palle out of jail.

"I'm sorry, Stan, I didn't know she was going to do that," I said. "I just wanted to get Palle out of jail. He didn't kill Troy."

"This isn't the way to go about it."

"I'll be right there," I said and hung up before he could respond.

So much for my smooth working relationship with the police.

CHAPTER

FIVE

I winked to an alley I knew just a block away from Mallory's precinct. The air was crisp and still held the last orange rays of the setting sun. A layer of snow covered the asphalt ground, turning the normal cracked surface into smoother lumps.

I headed for the precinct. A steady wind blew toward me, picking up the dusting of snow and sending it swirling around in eddies along the sidewalk. Jagged clumps of ice and snow lined the road where the snowplows had pushed them, exposing underbellies of dirt and salt.

The entrance to the precinct had been well shovelled and covered in dirt. I felt the grittiness as I stepped over it and pulled open the door.

I didn't recognize the officer on duty at the counter. He gave me a polite, disinterested nod as I asked for Detective

Mallory. He picked up the phone to make the inquiry and slowly the disinterested look faded as he focused in on me. By the end of the call, he was outright staring at me, his lips pressed tight together.

"You can go in," he said, gesturing to the metal detector to my right. "Go down the hall to the end. Turn left and then take the first right."

That wasn't the way to Mallory's cubicle in the detectives' pen. A feeling of impending disaster came over me. Had contacting the lawyers for Palle damaged my connection to Mallory completely?

Only one way to find out.

I passed through the detector without a beat and followed the directions the front desk officer had given me. The same mint green covered the walls as I passed the normal turnoff to the detectives' pen. Now the colour seemed to take on a slightly darker, more sinister hue. The air smelled a little staler, with an undercurrent of day old coffee and nervous sweat.

Or maybe that nervous sweat was just me.

By the time I reached the right door my body felt tense and on edge. I'd unwound my scarf and opened the throat of my coat to stop the strangled feeling I was having. The door knob felt clammy in my palm as I clenched it and turned. As I pushed I heard angry voices rising in volume.

The room was an interview room, different from one I'd been in before. The same mint green covered the walls but there was no mirrored wall denoting one way glass.

Instead of the table with a pair of hard back chairs, the room held two beige fabric couches, one on the far wall and the other set against the left wall. They looked only slightly more comfortable than the hard backed chairs were which was maybe why Mallory and a woman in a navy suit stood in the centre of the room, facing off against each other.

Both stood with arms crossed, one leg forward and the other back, as if they were about to launch into fisticuffs. Instead of his usual bland expression, Mallory looked angry. Brows drawn down, his lips pressed so hard together they almost disappeared into his face, leaving just the slash of his mouth.

The woman seemed to match him with anger. She had cropped black hair, combed forward into jagged points that framed her face. Scarlet lipstick decorated her mouth which was almost as pressed as tightly closed as Mallory's. She had brilliant blue eyes that glared with an icy stare. Although she only came up to his shoulders, she held herself erect with a no nonsense bearing. The navy suit looked tailored to her slim form. Her nails, clenching her arms, making the fabric crease, were well manicured and covered in a scarlet colour that matched the lipstick.

As I entered they both shut up and slowly turned to glare at me.

"Sorry I'm late," I announced to the room at large, as if they were expecting me. "Can you tell me what I missed?"

Both of them started speaking at once. Mallory's deep voice seemed to almost drown out the woman's voice until she took a deep breath and began projecting. Soon her curt, sharp tones cut through Mallory's voice.

"I came down here at your request to get bail for Mr. Gudbrand and this *detective* has been giving me nothing but the runaround."

"I'm merely tried to get confirmation from your so-called client and he said he didn't know you."

"And I told you my firm was hired by Mr. Kringle to represent Mr. Gudbrand," the woman snapped.

Mallory opened his mouth to respond but I jumped in first.

I moved across the room, holding out my hand toward the woman.

"I'm Noel Kringle," I said. "I assume you're from Rutherford, Henderson, Judges, and Sloan."

"Yes, that's right." She uncrossed her arms then gripped my hand and gave me a firm shake. "I'm Nadia Judges. I've been trying to get in to see my client and this detective..."

"Yes, I caught the gist of it," I said. "I didn't let Palle know to expect you, nor did I have a chance to let the police know either." I gestured to Mallory. "I'm sure Detective Mallory will be happy to have one of his officers bring up Palle so you can talk with him."

I glanced back at Mallory with my eyebrows raised. I sent him a mental pretty please. A muscle along his jaw jumped but he moved to the door and called through for an officer.

"Bring up Palle Gudbrand and put him in interrogation room two," he said. "His *lawyer* wants to talk to him." He gave the word 'lawyer' the same snide emphasis that Judges had given to 'detective.'

When I looked back at her, I noticed the narrowing of her eyes as she looked past me at Mallory. I knew if I didn't head her off there was going to be another round of angry retorts.

"Perhaps I can have a few moments alone with Ms Judges," I said.

Mallory shrugged. "Fine by me." He turned and left the room, pulling the door closed then giving it a jerk to slam it shut the last two inches.

"Exasperating," Judges said. "I've been trying to see Mr. Gudbrand and not getting anywhere for over half an hour. I usually send an associate for this but your family has always been one of our top level clients. I don't appreciate this runaround."

"I didn't realize you were coming right down," I said. "If you'd let me know..."

"I've never had a *detective* be so rude," she continued as if I'd never spoken. She looked past me toward the door where Mallory had exited. "He kept insisting that Mr. Gudbrand hadn't retained us so I couldn't speak to him."

"Well, Palle didn't know...," I said.

"I am really considering a complaint," she said, still not looking at me. "My time is valuable."

I took a breath. Had this woman even heard a word I'd said? She was supposed to be working for me.

I focused on her. Soon the image of her favourite Christmas present flowed into my mind. A pair of white, laced ice skates. She had wanted to be a figure skater but wasn't coordinated enough.

Another breath and I let the image go but I carried the knowledge in my voice.

"My time is valuable as well," I said. "Perhaps if we focused instead of arguing in cross purposes you might have more time in your life for skating lessons."

She started, her head jerking around. She stared at me, eyes wide. For a moment, I could see the young girl inside, uncertain of herself, of how to move her feet on skates, trapped with the bounds of a highly competent, controlled woman. Then the wall closed down. She pulled herself even more erect.

"Of course, I didn't mean to imply your time wasn't valuable, Mr. Kringle," she said.

"Good," I said. "I'll confirm with Palle that I hired you for him and then we can get it taken care of."

She nodded.

I crossed to the door and let myself out.

Palle was just coming down the hall, flanked by two police officers. His hands were cuffed behind his back. His expression was somber and distant but as soon as he spotted me, he perked up. His head lifted and his eyes cleared. I caught a flicker of light-green skin on his forehead before it vanished beneath regular human skin.

As he drew closer, I nodded to him.

"I hired a lawyer for you, Palle," I said. "She inside. Just talk with her and do what she says. We'll get you out of here."

He opened his mouth to respond then closed it again. A breath huffed out of his barrel chest. He nodded then dropped his gaze as the officers steered him past me and through the door. A moment later they returned and took up watch on either side of the door.

I turned to find Mallory standing in the middle of the hall, arms crossed.

"Kringle, you and I have to talk."

He whirled and started walking, not even waiting to see if I followed.

I hurried to catch up.

He took me through several twists to another interrogation room. This one, like the one for Palle, didn't have the one way glass on any wall. It also didn't contain any couches or any chairs at all. Instead, the ten foot square space was empty and smelled slightly stale, like it wasn't used much. Even the mint green paint looked a little faded, like it hadn't had a fresh coat when all the other walls had.

When the door clicked shut behind me, Mallory turned to face me. His knuckles whitened against his shirt where he gripped his arms.

Before he could open his mouth, I jumped in.

"I'm sorry Stan, really I am. I didn't know the lawyer was going to get here so fast. I would have given you a heads up if I'd known. I just wanted to get Palle out of here as soon as possible."

He blew out a long breath. A slight frown remained on his face but I noticed his knuckles weren't quite so white any more.

Now if he would only uncross his arms.

"I don't appreciate being jumped by an attorney," he said. "I thought we had an understanding."

"We do," I said. "But I also know that Palle didn't kill Troy Bengali and you know it too."

"He was right there," Mallory said. "You said so yourself."

"So were the security guards," I said. "They didn't see anything. And you know things can happen that you can't explain in your police reports."

He sighed. His arms loosened. He shook his head.

"Why does it always have to be weird stuff with you, Kringle?" he asked.

"Just lucky I guess."

His lips twitched but he didn't let himself smile. He opened his mouth to reply when the door behind me opened.

A uniformed officer stuck his head in.

"We've got another body, sir. Like the others."

Mallory's mouth snapped shut with a hard click. His face twisted into a grimace.

Wait, others, plural?

Before I could ask, Mallory moved past me and headed for the door.

"We'll finish later," he said, not even glancing back.

The door closed with a soft click, leaving me with stuffy air and faded mint green walls.

Others? Troy Bengali wasn't the first?

Wasn't this supposed to be the most wonderful time of the year?

WHEN I LEFT THE INTERROGATION ROOM IT ONLY TOOK A FEW moments before I found an officer who could direct me back to where I'd left Palle and the lawyer Nadia Judges. By the time I got back, Palle was already heading back down the hall, followed by two officers. Nadia Judges stood just outside the door, staring at her smart phone screen. She looked up as I approached.

"Where's Palle going?" I said. My heart started to beat a little faster as he moved away. Hadn't she been able to get him bail?

"They're returning him to his cell for the moment," she said. "Don't worry, it won't be for long. I just have to get an order signed by the judge then he'll be out on bail. It should only take me a short time."

"How short?" I asked.

"He'll be out tonight," she said. "I promise." Her voice took on a distracted tone as she looked back at her phone.

I wanted to ask for a time but I held back. I had already

had to mollify Mallory, I didn't want to have to do it again with the lawyer.

"So I'll wait for your call?" I asked.

"Uh huh." She waved a hand in my general direction as she started to move away, following the same direction that Palle had taken.

Soon I was alone in the hall, surrounded by mint green walls.

I went to find out where Mallory had gone. I had a sneaking suspicion that this other death might have something to do with Troy Bengali.

It sounded like there was weirdness happening and what better place to be that smack dab in the middle of it.

CHAPTER

SIX

I looked for Mallory but couldn't find him and ended up back at the front counter. The same officer stood there, a young man reviewing reports. He glanced over as I exited through the metal detector. I came around the other side of the counter and leaned on it.

The last of the sunshine was coming through the windows behind me but it was weak compared to the yellowish overhead lights. On most people it made their faces look washed out and ghastly but the young officer had a tinge of olive in his skin, giving him a healthy glow.

He glanced up with a quizzical look when I leaned across the counter toward him.

"Did you receive a call for Detective Mallory?" I asked.

"I'm sorry, sir, I can't discuss police business," he said.

"Of course, I understand." I focused on him. He was a little more opaque. Influencing him would take some effort.

But even as I thought that, I could feel myself sinking into my magic. It made everything resonate around me. I caught a faint hint of ammonia left over from the most recent cleaning. It reminded me of the Elves frantically disinfecting the back of the sleigh in preparation for the Christmas Eve journey. The worn counter recalled the long worktables in the Elves' workshop.

I looked up into the young officer's eyes. They were light brown, almost hazel. For a moment, he was looking right at me, then I saw his gaze defocus. He was looking past me, looking away, far away, into the past.

To his favourite Christmas present.

I caught a hint of pine and the cold, crisp taste of air rushing past. My hands tightened as if gripping something, a rubber handle on top of...

Poles.

I felt my legs bend. My body hunched over. Focusing on speed, being aerodynamic. Racing down a hill.

Skis. His favourite present had been a pair of downhill skis.

"By the way," I said. "You wouldn't happen to know where Detective Mallory went, do you?"

His mouth dropped open, ready to reply that it wasn't my concern.

"Those red skis were really nice," I said.

A smile spread over his face. He suddenly looked

younger. He held his hand out on the counter, loosely curled, as if he was holding a pole in each.

Now. He would never be more suggestible.

"Detective Mallory?" I asked.

"He got called away to a homicide at 1214 Castle Park Drive," said the officer. "Third famous one this week."

I had started to release my influence but stopped at his last comment. "What do you mean third famous one?"

"First Billy Wattle on Sunday, then Troy Bengali yesterday, now Suzanne Delson today."

I stared at the young officer. Billy Wattle was a famous Toronto DJ who was still popular during the morning drive time, even in this era of satellite radio. Troy of course had been famous for his foundation, and Suzanne Delson was a TV host of a popular daytime current events and styles show.

Three in less than a week?

"You've been very helpful," I said. "You should deal with your work now."

He nodded and shifted away from me. I retreated out of the police station until I was outside in the fresh, cold air. Even as the breeze ruffled my hair and I wrapped my scarf around my neck, I felt a chill that had nothing to do with the temperature weedle its way up my spine.

Troy's death hadn't been a random event. And while murder in a city this size wasn't surprising, the death of so many well known people in so short a time had to mean something.

Just as I was about to *wink* my way to Castle Park Drive I

heard the faint tinkling of my cell phone. I pulled it out of coat and flipped it open.

"Kringle," I said.

"Mr. Kringle, it's Stella Masterson," the voice of Troy Bengali's executive assistant sounded faint and tearful in my ear. "The police have confiscated all of the toys from the Toy Stash. Please can you help us get them back? Troy would want the donation drive to go on and I just don't know how..."

Her voice broke off and I heard a broken sob on the other end of the phone.

"I'll take care of it, Stella, don't you worry about it," I said.

"Oh, thank you, Mr. Kringle. I know Troy would be very upset if something happened with the Toy Stash donations."

I assured her again I would deal with it and let her go before she started sobbing over the phone.

I stuffed the phone back into my pocket. The last rays of the sun was gone, leaving the growing darkness. Cars streamed by, tossing up pieces of slush. A moment later, the street lights flickered on, glowing a soft yellow and reflecting off the piles of snow beside the road like sparkling jewels.

I had my hands in the pockets of my navy pea coat and only became aware of how they were clenched into fists. My whole body felt tight with tension. What had started as a delightful job guarding donated toys had turned into a nightmare of murder. And not only that, now the toy donations were threatened.

Now I really had a reason to find Mallory at 1214 Castle Park Drive.

I DIDN'T KNOW THE AREA WELL SO IT TOOK MORE ENERGY TO *WINK* there. A dull headache bloomed in my temples when I landed at the corner of Lawrence and Castle Park Drive. As I headed north along the road, fat, fluffy snow flakes started to fall. Around me stretched out large expanses of lawns, covered in blankets of pristine snow. Most of the lawns had rows of hedges or walls surrounding them but they were now almost indistinguishable under the snow.

The houses sat farther back, lights in windows reminded me of Christmas balls glittering on a tree. Many of the houses topped three storeys. A few were even four storeys.

They didn't call this the rich section of town for no reason.

The sidewalk was perfectly cleared with dirt scattered around for traction. The ground rose slightly as I followed the path. Ahead of me, above the rise, flickering lights glowed.

As I crested the top, I saw four police cruisers parked at angles across the road. The lights on top of the hoods flashed red and blue. In the middle of the space, parked in the driveway of one of the three storey houses was an ambulance.

Officers in coats and gloves created a perimeter around the area. I slowed my approach to study the house.

It was grey brick with cream shutters. Two columns in front gave it a faux Roman appearance although the roof looked like a typical arch with slate tiles. The coloured lights from the police cars flickered against the windows, reflecting like a kaleidoscope.

A cluster of people huddled between the columns. I picked out the cropped hair of Stan Mallory in the centre.

Now I just have to get down to talk to him.

I started forward again but only managed to get halfway to the police car before an officer stepped out from the road to intercept me.

"Excuse me, sir, this is an active investigation. I'll have to ask you to cross to the other side of the street if you wish to get through."

In the flickering light, I caught a glimpse of an Asian face under the brim of his police hat. He wore a bulky, police jacket that ended at his hips. From his legs and arms, I could tell the bulkiness probably came from a bulletproof vest and wasn't his natural build.

"I don't need to get through," I said. "I'd like to speak to Detective Mallory when he's available. Please tell him it's Noel Kringle."

The man gave a dispassionate nod before he turned away. He lifted his hand to his mouth and I heard him murmur to himself. It took me a moment to realize he was talking into a radio.

I watched as Mallory detached himself from the group and stalked across the lawn in my direction. Instead of walking down the drive and then the sidewalk, he cut across the pristine blanket of snow, leaving a broken trail behind him. His boots kicked up puffs of snow ahead of him. Fortunately, unlike the other lawns, this one didn't have a wall or hedge around it, so Mallory reached the sidewalk without trouble.

He waved away the officer before turning back to me.

"Noel, what the hell are you doing here?" he asked.

"Suzanne Delson, third one this week," I said. "It's only Wednesday, Stan, and you've got three prominent Toronto figures dead. Don't you think you might need my help with this?"

"This one might not even be a murder. It looks accidental. And even if it is murder, it doesn't have anything to do with your kind of weirdness."

Annoyance flushed his face but it might also have been the flickering red lights.

"Okay, maybe so," I conceded. "But you've confiscated the toys from the Toy Stash. The Bengali Foundation needs them to continue the toy drive. When will they get them back?"

"When we finish with the investigation, Noel. Really I thought you'd figure that out."

"They're toys for needy kids, Stan. Can't you guys do your forensic tests on them and release them?"

He opened his mouth, then closed it and shook his head.

"Come on, Stan, there's got to be something you can do."

He took a step closer to me, ducking his head.

"There's a lot of heat on these ones, Noel. I can't do anything out of the ordinary. Everything by the book here. I'm sorry, I'd like to help. I know where those toys go. I gave a few of them myself but I can't get them released without a judge's say so and no judge is going to release them before a trial."

A trial. That would take years. This year's donations would be devastated by the loss. We'd never gather enough toys to cover the families who had been chosen.

"Sorry, Noel."

I blew out a breath, watching my breath turn to mist.

"Okay, I've got a proposition for you. I'll find a way to replace all the toys but I want in on the investigation. Troy Bengali was my client and a friend. Palle is my associate and also my friend and I want a chance to prove he's innocent before he's railroaded for the rest of these 'incidents'. You let me in and I'll make sure there's no leak to the press about the police holding onto those toys and ruining some needy families' Christmas."

"Noel, you wouldn't do that."

"Wouldn't I?" I said. "You know I don't want to cause you trouble, Stan, but this is Palle. And I have a feeling there really *is* something strange going on with these murders. Didn't you say I'm always involved in the weird ones?"

Mallory folded his arms across his chest. "That wasn't something to aspire to."

"You know it's true in this case. Otherwise you wouldn't have said it." I nudged his elbow. "Come on, Stan, you know I can help you. I can ask the questions and look in places you can't. I'm going to do it anyway, this way you'll hear what I've got. But only if you tell me what you've got."

His lips pressed tight together but I could see a slight curve upward at the ends. But it might also have been shadows from the flickering lights.

"Okay. Come by the office tomorrow morning and I'll bring you up to speed," he said. "But you only talk to me and you make sure there's no bad publicity about the Toy Stash."

"I promise," I said.

We shook on it then he turned away. This time he walked back along the sidewalk to the driveway.

The front door opened, spilling light out between the two columns. The sound of voices rose up, carrying across the snow. I heard the clatter of metal and then a man started walking backwards, pulling something along with him. A metal gurney. On top of it rested a long, black bag.

I turned away and started back up the rise toward Lawrence. I didn't need another glimpse of the body bag.

By the time I returned to my office, it was almost seven. To avoid making my headache worse, I'd taken the subway and then the streetcar across to my office building. It was a small, six storey with a decrepit elevator that made walking up the four flights to my office an attractive idea most of the time.

I kicked the snow off my boots and trudged up the stairs to my floor. By the time I got there, I felt pleasantly warm, enough so that I unwound my scarf and unbuttoned my coat.

When I reached the door, I noticed light coming through the frosted glass, highlighting the engraved SC Private Investigations. I grabbed the door knob. It turned easily in my hand.

Inside, I spotted the left half of Venir's back. He was sitting in one of the hard back chairs in front of my desk.

Not my desk chair.

He had to be really feeling out of sorts if he wasn't trying to sneak into my chair every chance he got. He claimed it was for comfort but I knew he liked the idea of sitting behind the desk.

Now he wasn't even making an effort.

Maybe I could do something about that.

I cleared my throat. His pointed ear twitched.

"Venir, I've got an important job for you."

SEVEN

The ear twitched again and this time he turned around in the chair. The unlit cigar hung from the corner of his mouth.

"What's that, boss?" he asked.

I shrugged off my coat and dumped it on the sagging brown sofa as I walked by. I skirted around the end of my desk and sank into my leather chair. It felt nice to sit after standing around for hours.

"First things first," I said. "Were you able to find anything that would affect Palle?"

He shook his head. "Sorry, kiddo, no go. There's nothin' here that would cause a troll to miss seeing something like a body. I didn't check the Magical Realms." He gave a shrug.

I nodded. Unless we had an idea of where to look, it

could take months or even years to search the entire multi-dimensions of the Magical Realms.

"You didn't feel any trace of magic near the Toy Stash?" I asked.

The Elf shook his head. His white curls bobbed on his head. "Nope, nothing at all. It was like it didn't happen."

If only it hadn't. I would have given almost anything not to have seen Troy Bengali's foot sticking out from under the Toy Stash.

"Okay, drop that thread for now. We'll get back to it," I said. "I've got a lawyer working on getting Palle out on bail. He might be able to give us more to go on when he's free. For now, I've got another job I need you to do."

Venir took the cigar out of his mouth and held it in his hand as he rested both hands on his knees. "What's that, boss?"

"All the toys in the Toy Stash have been confiscated by the police for their investigation. Mallory says they probably won't be released until the trial which could be years away and that's after they catch whoever did it. Meanwhile, the Bengali Foundation has an obligation to those needy families. And we're going to help them."

Venir nodded again. He leaned forward to catch my every word.

"I'm putting you in charge of replacing those toys," I said. "You were a Christmas Elf, you should have no problem finding a way to make those toys."

I leaned back, pleased with myself. I'd suspected Venir's

growing melancholy was because he wasn't at the North Pole building toys. I remembered the joy and delight on the Elves' faces as they worked. They lived to create and build toys for children. They would do it all day long if they could. I remembered how my mother had instituted mandatory breaks for breakfast, lunch, and dinner, as well as a break mid-morning and mid-afternoon so the Elves wouldn't burn themselves out. Several had tried to resist, saying they didn't need so many breaks but my mother insisted. And sure enough, output increased even as their workday shortened.

Thinking about those smiling faces now, I knew Venir would be happy to get the chance to do the work he'd been born to do again.

But instead of a smile spreading across his face, he scowled at me. His face turned beet red. He jumped off the chair, landing on both feet with a thump. His hands tightened into fists, clenched so hard, pieces of the crushed cigar trickled from between his fingers.

"I am *not* building toys," he snarled. "I am *not* having anything to do with toys. You want someone to do that, you get yerself another Elf, Kringle."

He glared at me then flicked his left hand up and vanished, leaving only a few pieces of shredded cigar that floated down to the floor.

I stared at the empty space where Venir at been standing a moment before.

I had misread the situation. Boy, had I ever. He'd never spoken to me that way before. I'd never seen him so angry.

"Venir, I'm sorry," I said out loud. I projected my voice through the office. "I made a mistake. I'm really sorry."

No response. Nothing.

I'd screwed up, big time.

Would he even come back?

He had first appeared with dire warnings about someone wanting to kill my dad and helped me stop a rogue faerie bent on destroying the peace negotiated by my dad between the Faerie Courts of Winter and Summer in the Magical Realms. He'd then decided to join my company and, while he could sometimes be an annoyance, I'd grown to like having him around.

The thought of him leaving for good saddened me more than I would have thought.

And if he did, it was my fault because I'd completely misread the situation.

Damn the halls.

A knock sounded on the door from the hall. I jumped out of my chair and hurried around my desk. Maybe it was Venir, although why he wouldn't just *wink* into the office, I didn't know. Maybe he wanted to be formal, demand a formal apology from me.

I'd give it to him. I owed him that. Then maybe later, after a few months, I would actually ask him what was wrong as opposed to assuming I knew.

But as I approached the door I realized the shadow outside was too large to be Venir.

I opened the door.

Palle stood in the hall. He appeared as his troll self. His shoulders hunched and his head bowed so he wouldn't put it through the ceiling if he straightened. Dark circles deepened his eyes. His tusks almost drooped in his mouth then I realized he was frowning.

"I am sorry I have brought shame onto you, Noel," he said.

"You did nothing of the sort, Palle. Come in."

I held the door open as he entered. He filled the space in my waiting room, making everything look like miniatures. Standing, he was still hunched over, head bowed forward.

"Please sit down, Palle," I said.

Gently, he lowered himself onto the sofa. He took up the entire length of it but surprisingly it didn't sag any more than normal. It seemed accustomed to his weight.

I grabbed one of the yellow plastic chairs and pulled it over to sit on. I placed it directly in front of Palle and settled in.

"Let's go over everything from last night," I said.

"There is not much to tell," Palle said. "It was quiet. I stood in front of the Toy Stash near the wall for much of the evening. Sometimes I would move to stand by the window. Once the security guards offered me some coffee which I declined."

"Which one offered you the coffee?" I asked.

"I do not recall his name," Palle said. "He was young I believe. His hair was darker than the other man's."

As a troll, Palle sometime had difficulty distinguishing one human from another but he was getting better at it.

I remembered when I signed in yesterday afternoon. There had been an older security guard, about fifty, who had had me sign in and another, younger man watching the monitors. He was probably the one who had offered Palle a coffee. I would have to get his name so I could talk to him.

"Okay, after the guard offers you coffee and you declined what happened?" I asked.

Palle shook his head. "Nothing. The rest of the night was quiet. No one came in. No one approached the Toy Stash. I moved from the window to the wall and back."

"No one came near," I said. "You're sure? Did you feel anything in the air? Smell anything?"

Another head shake. "It was the same as every night, except in the front lobby instead of the back."

"Did you feel sleepy at all? Zone out at any point?"

"No, I don't believe so," Palle said. "But I must have done so. I obviously shirked my duty."

"You did not shirk your duty, Palle," I said. "Something happened. I don't know what and I don't know how but I'm going to figure it out. I know you didn't kill Troy. I going to find out who did. Now what did the lawyer say?"

"I am out on bail," the troll said. "I cannot leave the city. I am to report to the police every afternoon."

"Okay, you do what you're supposed to do. Follow the lawyer's advice and try not to worry."

"I am sorry I brought shame on the company, Noel."

I patted one of his large knees. My hand barely covered half of it.

"Don't worry about it," I said.

Palle glanced around. "Where is Venir?"

"Ah, he's off for the moment," I said. "One thing you could do is write down any spells or creatures that can affect you. I'll check back in."

I got up from the chair and went into my office. I grabbed my special notebook that was sitting on my desk blotter. My mother had given it to me, along with a stapler, pen, and paperclip holder. The notebook magically transferred any notes I made in it onto my computer and even erased itself when a case was finished. I'd also found that if I tore out a page, any writing on that page appeared in the notebook, added to the specific case the writing referred to.

I tore out a page, grabbed a pen and carried them out Palle.

"Use this," I said. "Take your time. Write down everything you can think of, no matter how obscure."

"Of course, Noel." He took the paper and pen from me.

"I'll be back in a little while," I said.

He nodded. He reached across to the chair I'd been sitting in. With a flick of his finger, he drew it toward him and set the paper down on the seat. The pen looked like a toothpick in his hand as he bent over to start writing.

I left him to it, and *winked.*

I landed a block away from the Bengali Foundation. If I was lucky, the two guards from the night before would be on duty and I could interview them. They had probably already talked to the police and might be skittish. I just hoped my previous association with Troy Bengali made them a little more willing to talk to me.

I didn't want to have to resort to any Christmas influencing. I would never be able to completely trust the information. It might be true or they just might be trying to please me.

The snow was falling more steadily now, fat flakes drifting and dancing in the swirling wind. I could feel the hint of ice pellets in the air. It was just humid enough and cold enough to create that unusual blend.

Snow and ice crunched under my feet as I walked. King Street was silent and still. Ahead of me, the traffic lights flicked from red to green, signalling to nothing. In the distance behind me I heard a grating sound. I glanced back and caught sight of a lone streetcar rumbling along but it was still several blocks away.

I crossed the street and climbed the granite steps up to the Bengali Building. White light blazed from the windows. When I reached the double glass doors, I pulled on them and found them locked. Just to the right was a buzzer so I pressed it.

Through the glass, I saw a lone security guard at the front desk. It was the older one from the night before. I lifted my hand in a wave. He gave a nod. A moment later, a buzzing sounded from the door. I grabbed the handle and pulled the door open.

Warmth from the lobby made me gasp. The change in temperature was a shock. I unwrapped my scarf from around my neck.

To my left, the space where the Toy Stash had been was empty. Not even a single toy remained although they had left the sign behind. It looked sad and forlorn sitting on the granite floor all by itself. The Toy Stash, sponsored by the Bengali Foundation, security by SC Private Investigations, Noel Kringle, President.

Some security.

I am going to find your killer, Troy. I promise.

I walked over to the security desk. The guard was already standing, the clipboard slid across the counter. He held out the pen for me to sign in.

"I don't need to sign in," I said. "I was hoping to talk to you about last night if I could."

The guard pursed his lips. "The police said I shouldn't talk to anyone."

"I appreciate that," I said. "I was working for Mr. Bengali, providing security for the Toy Stash." I gestured at the empty space behind me.

"I'm aware," the guard said. He kept his tone carefully neutral.

"I also consider him a friend," I said. "I'd like to help find whoever did this."

"Seems to me the police think your employee did it," the guard said.

"They have that suspicion," I said. "Did you or your partner see anything last night that would make you think that?"

A frown creased his mouth. "My partner?"

"Yes, the young man watching the monitors."

The guard shook his head. "There was no one else here last night. There never is. I do the night shift on my own."

I stared at him and then glanced over. I remembered seeing the younger man sitting right there, his head bowed as he looked at something just below the counter level. I had assumed he was watching security monitors. But thinking about it, I never saw the older guard looking over at him and they never had any interaction that I saw.

Yet I had seen him and so had Palle. He had even offered Palle some coffee.

"Do you mind if I just check something?" I said to the guard. He gave me a puzzled look but didn't say anything. I moved around the desk to my right, aiming for the spot where I'd seen the younger guard. Just as I reached the edge to step behind the desk, the older guard reacted.

"I don't think so," he said, holding out his hand to stop me.

"I won't touch anything," I said. I held my hands up to chest level. "See? I just want to look."

"Well, as long as you don't touch anything."

I stepped around the desk and stood beside him. Below the counter level, the desk area held a row of monitors, showing several angles of the elevators and the front and back lobbies. Every few moments the images flickered and changed, shifting to different views. I assumed some of them were from the floors above us.

To the far right, in front of the guard, sat a white mug of coffee on top of a folded newspaper. A glass jar full of pens were tucked in between two of the monitors. In between another pair was a crossword puzzle book. But all of these items were closer to the right side, where the older guard sat. There nothing near the left side where I stood.

I took a deep breath and opened my inner senses. Instantly, everything around me sharpened. I smelled a faint whiff of ammonia still lingering on top of the counter. It mingled with the spiciness of the older guard's aftershave and the musk scent of his deodorant. The hum of the elevators sharpened as they moved up and down the shafts. The tick of the clock hanging on the wall above our heads sounded as loud as a gong. I could even tell how much milk had been added to the guard's coffee.

And under all of it, I felt the telltale tingle of residual magic, vibrating just below the threshold of awareness, like a background hum.

I took another step closer to the desk. The tingle

strengthened, running along my skin like static electricity. The tone of it felt familiar, like I'd been exposed to it before but I didn't recognize it. It didn't feel like Venir or Palle. But there was something definitely familiar about it. I just couldn't quite put my finger on it.

But it did tell me one thing. Someone magical had been here last night. I'd seen him and so had Palle. He was powerful enough to mask himself from a regular human and strong enough to hide around other magical beings by cloaking himself in a persona that matched his surroundings. I had little doubt now that whatever it was had killed Troy Bengali and stuffed his body underneath the mound of toys right in front of Palle without Palle being aware of it.

That kind of power was almost unprecedented. Only a few creatures had it.

And I sure wasn't one of them. Even at the North Pole, I didn't have that kind of magic.

But that wasn't going to stop me from finding whoever it was.

I stepped back out from behind the desk.

"Thanks for that," I said to the security guard. "If it would be okay with you, I may need to ask you some more questions later."

"Well I suppose," he said. "Are you sure your guy didn't do it?"

"Did you see him do it?" I asked. "You were here the entire time, same as him. Did you see him do anything remotely like it?"

The frown deepened on the man's face. "Well no. But I wasn't really paying attention to him. I watch the monitors when there isn't anyone to sign in."

"But you would have seen Palle if he dragged Mr. Bengali's body out of the elevator," I said.

"Well, yeah, I suppose I would have noticed that."

"You probably would have even seen it on the elevator too," I said. "Him bringing down the body. Did you see that?"

"No." He said the word reluctantly. He tipped his head down as if he was looking at the monitors.

"Do you keep recording of what's on there?" I asked.

"The police have them," he said.

"Okay. I'll check with them. Thanks for your help."

He gave me a distracted nod, still not looking up from the monitors. The frown still played on his mouth but at least it wasn't directed at me anymore. I'd introduced questions into his mind with my questions about seeing Palle with Troy. Would those questions be enough to dissipate the fog of magic that had obscured what he had really seen?

I would have to give him time to work that out and check back. Meanwhile, I would have to get Palle thinking about it too. He might be able to penetrate any magic obscuring his memories faster than the security guard.

Then I had to find a way to replenish the Toy Stash and find a way to apologize to Venir.

It was going to be a long night.

CHAPTER

EIGHT

By the time I got back to my office, Palle was gone. He had left the paper on my desk blotter. His neat printing filled almost the entire page. After hanging up my coat and scarf on the nail attached to the back of my office door, I sat down in my leather chair to review it.

It was a thorough description of his night from his arrival to when Venir and I relieved him into the morning. It included a description of the older guard, right down the silver chain snaking out from his breast pocket. I remembered that it attached to a silver pocket watch, a memory that brought back the image of the boy playing with the train set. It had come unbidden to me when I signed in to see Troy yesterday afternoon. But nothing had come to me when I glanced over at the other, younger security guard.

I should have realized something was wrong at that

time. At this time of year it was all I could do to stop most people's favourite Christmas gift memory from popping into my mind. Being a desk width away from someone and not having it happen should have rung an alarm bell for me.

Some investigator I was.

But at least I could console myself that whoever it was had probably been trying to mask itself from me. I hadn't even been looking for anything wrong so why would I have noticed?

I'd be paying attention now, that was for sure.

At the very bottom of the report was a list of creatures that could influence trolls, including the spirit that had tricked Palle into crossing into the Human Realm. It was a very short list. I took the report and tucked it inside my notebook. By morning, it would be transcribed into my computer.

I leaned back in my chair and listened for the tell tale squeak of the wheels. It sounded soft and forlorn in the quiet of my office. I'd turned off the light in the waiting room just beyond my door so all I could see was a slightly lumpy suggestion of a couch against the right wall. The rest of the waiting room was shrouded in darkness.

I glanced at my laptop and was shocked to see it was already eleven thirty. Where had the evening gone? On one hand this day had passed in the blink of an eye, on the other hand it seemed to have lasted forever.

And I still had to find a way to replenish the toys for the Toy Stash.

How was I going to do that? Obviously asking Venir had been a bust. I was going to have to do it on my own but how?

My brain didn't seem to want to function. Maybe I should go to a local toy store and just buy a bunch of things. If I explain why, maybe they would even give me a discount or pitch in some extra ones for free.

Okay, that was one possibility. I had to come up with at least one more so I would have options if something fell through.

Nothing else came to mind. I had to find a way to get my brain working.

I pushed up from behind my desk and grabbed my empty coffee mug as I moved around the right side. A while ago Venir had added a Keurig coffee machine to the small card table just outside the bathroom. A steaming cup might just be enough to keep me going.

I stepped through the office doorway into the waiting room. The brown couch was still a large lump sitting against the wall to my right. I fumbled along the wall to my left, hunting for the light switch. After a moment, my questing fingers felt nothing then my index finger bumped into the upraised switch. I flicked it.

Nothing happened.

I flicked it again, then several times. Still nothing.

The light bulb in the overhead light must have burned out.

I sighed and turned back to my office to set my cup back down on the desk before I tried to deal with light bulb.

The door swung shut in my face, plunging me into darkness.

Then I felt the telltale tingle of magic against my skin.

Something or someone was in the room with me. And from the menace I was starting to feel radiating around me, they didn't have good intentions.

My hand tightened on the coffee mug as the buildup of magical energy prickled against my skin. In the dark I couldn't tell where it was coming from, it seemed to come from all around me.

The prickling intensified, becoming a burning cold sensation. It reminded me of the worst snow storms at the North Pole. Filled with hurricane force winds, whipping snow squalls into fury. Ice shards as hard as metal and sharp as knives stabbing into my flesh like a million angry bees.

The cold, bitter and deep, seeping into my limbs, freezing my joints. The moisture in my eye balls froze. I closed my eyes, felt the crust along my eyelids crumble as I tried to blink.

Sharp and jagged burning with cold seemed to slash my lungs as I took a breath. I tried to cough but didn't have enough breath to spare. My diaphragm spasmed. I doubled over, feeling my muscles clench and grind against the cold.

Every part of me was freezing. I lost sensation in my feet. I couldn't feel the coffee mug in my hand. My right hand had frozen in a half open position. If the mug had fallen from my fingers, my frozen ears wouldn't have heard it. It could still be in my hand, welded with cold to my flesh.

I could feel the cold creeping along my limbs. I felt light headed, as if my blood flow had become too sluggish to flow up to my brain. My bowels felt leaden with cold.

Any moment the cold would reach my heart and freeze it to a solid stop.

Sleepy. I felt so sleepy...

No!

I forced my eyes open. I felt eye lashes tear from my lids as they separated. The darkness still surrounded me, deep and impenetrable. But something was there. Something strong enough to use cold against me.

But I'd grown up at the North Pole. Cold was second nature to me. I couldn't let this creature use it against me. I wouldn't.

I breathed through my nose, forcing breath deeper and deeper in my lungs. Then I began tiny little movements of my body. A slow side to side shake, warming my muscles, getting the blood flowing again.

As I moved, I remembered all the times I had been cold growing up. Burrowing in the snow with KJ. Mucking out the reindeer barns. Hauling tracks of toys from the workshop to the loading area with the Elves.

And I remembered the warm glow of my mother's kitchen where she always had a pot of hot chocolate or apple cider warming on the stove. The roaring fire place in the living room that dad kept going all winter long.

As I shifted my head from side to side, my brain began to clear again. I felt the cold porcelain of the mug still in my hand. My toes began to tingle with pins and needles as they woke up.

Use cold against me would you?

I took another deep breath, breathing in the frigid air. It seemed to be coming from the corner beside the line of plastic chairs on the same side of the wall as the door to the hall.

I focused, gathering the meagre forces of my own magic. It wasn't up to a straight out battle with whatever was there but there was something I could do that it couldn't.

Another breath and I sent out my questioning tendrils.

What is your favourite Christmas present?

The sudden blast of cold vanished in a swirl of confusion. I could feel the creature struggling against my question, trying to find a way to avoid it. But already I could sense a response flowing into me. I caught a glimpse of freshly fallen snow under thin trucked trees. Empty branches stretched up above my head.

Then the image was gone before I could grab onto anything else. I felt a rush of a presence blast past me.

The door to my office flew open as a shadow in the shape of a human figure smashed into it. I caught a glimpse in the light from my office desk lamp. Then the bulb in the lamp popped, plunging my office into darkness.

But I felt the shadow man still moving.

Running away from me.

Running from my question.

Then the cold was gone. The normal heat of my office

flooded in. I stumbled forward on legs that still felt slightly numb. I hit the switch on the wall and the overhead light flickered on.

The waiting room around me was empty but I still felt the lingering energy from the creature who had been hiding in the darkness. Had this been the way it had killed Troy and the others?

I would have to ask Mallory to have the coroner check for signs of hypothermia. If it was magically induced, it wouldn't be obvious on the outside of the body.

My hands and face still felt slightly numb. I dropped the coffee mug on the table beside the Keurig machine and stumbled into the bathroom. I flicked on the light and turned the taps to hot. I plunged my hands into the scalding water and let it run for a few moments before scooping it into my palms. I lifted my cupped palms and splashed the steaming water onto my face.

The crust dissolved along my eyelids. Even my eyes felt better with the heat. Eyes closed, I scooped another double palm full of water and splashed my face, then I turned off the tap.

Water dripping from my chin, I opened my eyes to look at my reflection in the mirror.

My hair and my beard had grown another three or four inches and were completely white.

Again.

I was going to have to cut it and dye it again.

Burning coals.

By the time I finished with my hair and beard, I only managed about three hours of sleep. I didn't even bother to go home, just stretched out on the lumpy brown sofa for a nap.

Even though it didn't look as elegant as Troy Bengali's fixtures, it was a damn comfortable couch for sleeping.

I woke up just before seven. In the bathroom, I managed to clean myself up with a washcloth and soap. For probably the millionth time, I contemplated how I could install a shower but the room really didn't have the space for it. Maybe if I found a way to block off the corner beside it, the shower could attach to the same piping system as the sink.

Then, dressed in my underwear, I made myself some coffee and carried it into my office. I kept an additional set of clothes in my desk, in the bottom drawer on the right side. It was an enchanted drawer that I used to keep things I didn't want anyone to find or if I needed a place to store something that might be harmful if left unattended.

From the drawer, I pulled out a pair of dark brown cords, a khaki shirt, and a fresh pair of black socks. I then balled up my clothes from yesterday and shoved them into the drawer. Before closing it, I murmured a short incantation. It was a spell for cleaning and returning the clothes to my apartment. They would then displace a different set of clothes which would appear in the drawer for the next time I needed a clean set of clothes.

I slid the drawer shut and donned the clothes before taking a sip of my coffee. As I set the mug down on my desk blotter, I noticed the red button on my phone flashing.

Someone had called and left a message.

Could it be Venir?

He never really used the phone but maybe he had this time. Maybe he was willing to let me apologize.

I grabbed the phone and dialled in to pick up the message.

"Noel, when you get this message get your butt down to the station. Now."

Mallory's voice, sounding tense and angry. I checked the time of the message and saw he'd left it just after six am.

Uh oh. What had happened now?

I gulped down more of my coffee and dialled his direct line. It rang once and then was picked up.

"What?" Mallory's voice sounded even more gruff than his message.

"I'm heading over right now," I said. "I wanted you to know I was on my way."

"Where was your friend, Palle, last night?" he asked.

"He was in my office for a while, then he went home," I said. "Why?"

"And he was acting normally?" Mallory asked.

"Stan, what's going on?"

He huffed a breath out and cleared his throat.

"I've reviewed the security DVD from the Bengali Foundation lobby. It shows Palle dragging Troy Bengali out of an elevator and covering him in toys."

I felt my jaw drop open in shock. That was impossible. It had to be. Palle couldn't have killed Troy. It didn't make any sense.

"You'd better bring your friend in," Mallory was saying. "I can't guarantee his safety if my officers have to get him."

"Stan, this isn't Palle at all, it's something else. I know it."

"You do, huh? Tell me Noel, how do you know it."

"I want to see those DVDs for myself."

"You're not gonna see anything different on them, Noel." His voice was gentle, like he was trying to let me down easy. "Trust me on this."

"I need to see them for myself, Stan."

Mallory sighed in my ear.

"Fine. Come down. Look at the tapes. But you should really consider bringing your friend in, Noel. It's for the best."

"I'll see you soon," I said.

I hung up, not confirming or denying that I'd bring Palle in but I didn't want to, not yet. Putting the troll in a jail cell might just be more dangerous for him than leaving out him.

I gulped down the last of my coffee, grimacing at the cold, bitter dredges. It lingered like ashes in my mouth as I pulled on my coat and scarf.

I paused in the waiting room and looked around. The place seemed quiet and still. Too empty by half.

I might have to get used to it again.

I didn't think I was going to like it.

I cleared my throat and spoke aloud to the empty room.

"Venir, I'm heading down to Mallory's precinct. I'll be back later. I'd like to talk to you if you'd let me."

I waited as the sound of my voice faded away.

No reply. Nothing.

I sighed and tied the scarf around my neck before I headed down the stairs and out into the early morning rush hour.

CHAPTER

NINE

I took a streetcar and then the subway north. Jammed in with the crowd, I soon found myself getting warm as I stood squished against a pole in the centre of the subway car. All around me people stood in their winter coats, hats pulled off their heads, hanging onto their briefcases or knapsacks. Men and women in suits. Teenagers in jeans. Several with thin jean jackets, barely enough to keep out the cold.

Down the car, I noticed several other men and women without coats. They probably got off at one of the stops that led directly into their office building. Maybe they never went outside all day and traveled home the same way, avoiding the cold.

At Bloor, the hub station where people switched from the

north/south train to the east/west train and vice versa, a women entered pushing a large, black stroller. She had her pink winter jacket tucked into the pouch on the back between her arms. Her brown hair was piled on top of her head and clipped, with wisps of curls hanging down. Her face was round with a long, thin nose.

In the stroller, a toddler of two or three sat strapped in, eyes wide she looked around. She had light brown hair, just a shade lighter than her mother's, but with the same big curls. Her round face also mirrored her mother's but her nose was a little larger and flatter, probably from her father. She wore a little green coat with red bells embroidered on it.

Her expression was a little apprehensive surrounded by all these much bigger people. I could sense that she wasn't quite sure about this, not sure if she was going to start crying.

I shifted a little, moving a step away from the pole I was holding on to. My movement caught the little girl's attention and she looked up at me.

I smiled at her and let the full feeling of Christmas bloom into my smile.

Her little mouth dropped open. Her eyes widened on her face. She threw her hands up in surprise. Then delight took over as a smile blossomed on her face. She clapped her hands together.

"Santa!" she cried out.

Even over the buzz of muffled music and the quiet

chatter of people talking, her voice carried through the entire car. The mother flushed with embarrassment. She leaned over the stroller to pat her daughter's head.

"Settle down there, Patty," she said.

"Santa!" the girl yelled again.

She reached out with both hands and leaned out of the stroller.

Reaching for me.

Maybe using the full force of Christmas magic hadn't been such a good idea. I forgot how much stronger it was the closer we got to the actual day.

Her mother grabbed both her hands and pulled her back into the seat.

"I'm so sorry," she said in my general direction.

"That's okay," I murmured. I tried to shift away around the pole but there were too many people in the way.

The little girl was not to be denied.

"Santa," she insisted. "*SANTA!*"

This time she punctuated her yell with a wiggle as she squirmed to pull herself out from beneath the strap around her waist. It was fastened tightly and she'd never be able to get herself out unless she got her feet up on the seat and pushed herself up.

Her legs kicked and then she got one foot up on the seat. Then the second one.

A moment later, she was pushing herself up in the seat, sliding out from beneath the waist strap.

At the same time, the subway lurched, braking suddenly.

Halfway out of the seat, the girl pitched forward. Aiming head first for the floor.

I let go of the pole and lunged forward, arms out.

And caught her as she fell out of the stroller.

She lifted her head from my arms and giggled in my face. She smelled of talcum powder and smushed peas.

"Santa," she breathed into my face.

I tilted my head so no one would see my face around her head.

"Shh," I whispered. "Don't tell anyone."

Her lips pressed tight together but they couldn't stop the giggles.

Then her mother reached down, her hands wrapping around the girl's torso.

"Oh my god, Patty what are you doing?"

"She's okay," I said. "She just slipped out."

"Thanks so much," the woman said. "I don't know what's gotten into her. I promised to take her for a photo with Santa today and she's got Santa on the brain."

She tilted her head and studied me. "You know, you look like…"

The door chimed sounded and the doors slid open.

I stepped away, waving at the little girl.

"Have a nice visit," I said and slipped out the door behind a man carrying a briefcase.

The little girl waved as the doors slid closed. I caught a glimpse of her mother's face, still looking confused.

A narrow escape.

I headed for the escalator to take me up to street level. On the way, I glanced in the metal surface of the wall going by.

My hair and beard still looked brown. The dye job from last night was holding.

For now.

At the police station, the front desk clerk ushered me through and handed me off to another officer who led me deeper into the station. Instead of directing me to Mallory's cubicle, she brought me to a contained office with actual walls, painted, naturally, in mint green. She knocked on the inner door and stood back to let me enter.

Mallory sat at a long desk set against the left wall. A large monitor sat on it. His black pants were creased more than usual and his sleeves were unbuttoned, rolled up to his elbows. Stubble dotted his chin and cheeks. His eyes looked blood shot.

Three Styrofoam cups sat in front of him.

He'd been up all night, I realized.

He waved me in, motioning at another black, desk chair sitting against the back wall. I grabbed it and wheeled it over to his right side. I sat down as he lifted one of the cups in front of him. It didn't have anything left in it. He frowned and picked up the second one, then the third. All of them empty.

"Stan, you look like hell," I said.

"You would too if you'd been up almost thirty hours," he

growled. "I got this security DVD from the Bengali Foundation keyed up like you asked."

"I know what you're saying, he had nothing to do with it," I said. "There's something odd going on." I paused, wondering if I should mention the magical attack on me last night.

One look at his lined, tired face discouraged that.

It would only bring up questions that I couldn't answer, and in his worn out frame of mind, it was only liable to irritate Mallory further.

I gestured to the monitor. "Let's look at the recording."

He hit play and the monitor lit up. From the angle of the image, the camera was high up in the corner nearest the front door. It gave a view of the expanse of the lobby. The Toy Stash was to the left against the wall. The security desk was just off centre at the top of the frame. The two elevator bays were visible on either side of the security desk. If I squinted I could even see the far end of each one, leading toward the back lobby.

Standing in front of the Toy Stash, beside the sign, stood Palle in his human form. His hands were crossed in front of him. He had a casual look to him, but I could see him moving his head slightly as he scanned the area.

I glanced up at the security desk. Two guards sat behind the desk. One, the older man sitting almost in the centre of the desk. The other, younger, staring down below the counter as if looking at the monitors.

My heart began to pound. The second guard captured on camera. If he had been a magical projection, he wouldn't have appeared on the security tape.

Which meant he had actually been there, even though the first security guard didn't remember him.

But Palle did and so did I. What did we have in common that the other security guard didn't?

Magic.

The second guard had created a spell that would hide him from regular people and the persona of a security guard to blend in for any magic user.

That told me that whoever or whatever they were was clever and thought ahead.

"This is at the beginning of the night," Mallory said. "Now I'm going to jump about an hour before the approximate time of death for our vic. Then I'll run slightly faster so you don't have to spend hours here watching it in real time."

"Got it," I said.

He flicked the remote. The time stamp at the top right corner of the screen changed to three o'clock. The figures on the screen jerked slightly from side to side. Palle's head motions looked like he was watching a fast-paced tennis match as his head flipped from side to side. The first security guard seemed to jump from the centre of the desk to the right hand side and back again.

The second security guard was motionless. Frozen, even at high speed.

And I noticed the first security guard did not even look in that direction never mind move over there.

Finally when the counter reach four fifty-seven, the second security guard moved. He stood up in a slow, fluid motion then walked across the lobby toward Palle. After a moment with Palle, he moved to the second elevator bay and disappeared.

The counter in the top right corner clicked away ten minutes. The elevator door opened but nothing came out. I peered closer, almost pressed my nose to the screen but the angle wasn't good enough to see deeper into the elevator.

"Stop it," I said to Mallory. "Go back about ten minutes to when the second security guard leaves the desk."

"Second security guard?" Mallory said. "What are you talking about? There's only one guard at the desk."

I jerked my head around to stare at him. He was looking at me like I'd grown a second head.

"Go back and I'll tell you when to stop," I said.

He hit the back button. The DVD whirled back.

"Stop," I yelled.

He hit the button. The image froze on the screen. Plainly I could see the second security just starting to round the corner of the desk. The first guard was sitting at the centre of the desk, looking down.

"Describe the scene to me," I said to Mallory.

"What?" he said.

"Humour me," I said. "Tell me what you see."

He shook his head and sighed.

"Okay, there's the mound of toys. There's Palle. There's the security desk and the guard sitting behind it. There's the elevators on either side of the desk."

His finger slid past the second security guard. I watched his face carefully. His gaze defocused and slid by before focusing again.

Even on the DVD, whatever magic the creature was using was powerful enough to render him invisible.

Damn the halls, that was impressive.

"What if I told you I see a second security guard," I said to Mallory. I pointed at the screen. "He's right there. He walks over to Palle and speaks to him, then goes over to the elevator and disappears into it."

Mallory tilted his head at me.

"You're shitting me, aren't you, Noel?"

I shook my head.

"I want you to concentrate," I said. "Focus where I'm pointing my finger and really concentrate at that spot."

I lifted my hand and pointed at the second security guard.

Mallory leaned forward. His brow crinkled as he stared at the spot. His mouth tightened with effort.

But even as he concentrated, I could see his eyes defocusing. The magic was too strong for him to see through it.

Maybe if I helped.

I reached over and grabbed his upper arm. The fabric of his shirt felt gritty. His flesh was warm beneath it.

I focused on him. See it. See *it!*

Malloy gasped. "Hey, what?"

He sat back, breaking my grip on his arm.

"What?" I asked. "What did you see?"

"I thought I saw... I thought..."

"Hold on to it, Stan, don't let it slip away."

Sweat beaded on his forehead. Muscles twitched along his jaw line. He was fighting to remember, I could see it in his eyes.

"There was... something," he said. "I think it was a man."

"That's right," I said. "What did he look like? What was he wearing?"

The lines on his forehead deepened as his eyebrows drew together.

"He looked... he looked... horrible and I think...red." He shuddered. "Everything he wore was red. Flowing robes... dripping red."

He sagged back in his chair, overcome with the effort of remembering. His eyes slid halfway shut. His breathing became shallow.

I touched his arm. His skin was cold and clammy. Sweat dripped down his forehead and the sides of his face. Even his crew cut looked wilted.

"Stan?" I said.

He didn't respond. I shook his arm. He flopped a little in his chair but his eyes remained half closed, his breath still shallow.

Swirling snow, I never should have pushed him to remember. Not only had he seen through the mask hiding the creature from human view, he'd seen through the disguise worn to fool any magic user.

He'd seen right through to the creature's true form.

"Stan!" I shouted in his ear.

He twitched a little. His breath hitched and then started again but his eyes remained half closed.

I grabbed each one of the Styrofoam cups. Empty, empty, about a mouthful of coffee left in the last one.

It would have to do.

I tossed the liquid into Mallory's face.

It splashed across his eyes and cheeks. He came back to himself sputtering and dripping coffee from his nose.

"What the fuck, Kringle," he roared.

I dug in my pocket and came up with a napkin from my last bagel. I handed it to him.

"Here. Sorry about that, the cup slipped in my hand."

"Next time, slip somewhere else." He wiped cold coffee from his cheek. A droplet hung on the edge of his left eyebrow but refused to fall.

I wanted to sag in relief but I didn't want to draw Mallory's attention. I set the cup back on the desk.

"So what did you see on the screen?" I asked.

I didn't look over at him in case he noticed my question was anything but casual.

"Nothing," he said. "There's the toy mound, Palle, and the security guard."

Whatever he'd seen was gone from his memory. I wasn't going to try to get it back. Who knew what would happen to him if I did that. He might end up catatonic for good.

"Let's go forward again," I said.

He hit the button and the DVD started again. I watched again as the second security guard moved smoothly across from the desk to Palle, and then from Palle to the elevator. This time, I didn't tell Mallory to stop but let the DVD play on. The elevator doors opened again and still nothing appeared. The frame wavered and the doors closed. The second security guard appeared back at the desk.

Wait a minute.

There had been a flicker in the frame.

"Stop and go back again about five minutes," I said. "Let it run at normal speed this time."

Mallory grunted but did as I asked.

The DVD started again. This time the second security guard moved faster than before, stopping briefly at Palle before moving to the elevator. About a minute passed before the elevator doors opened again. I stared at the screen, not blinking.

It flickered.

The second security guard, whoever he was, had done something to the DVD. He'd known he was being recorded and had used it to his advantage.

Suddenly Mallory hit the button and the image froze.

"I'm sorry Noel, that proves it."

"What?" I looked over at him, startled. "What are you talking about?"

He pointed at the screen. "There. Palle carrying Bengali out of the elevator and covering him with toys."

He pushed back from the desk and stood up. "You need to have Palle come in now."

I glanced back at the screen. To me, Palle was still standing frozen beside the sign. He hadn't moved other than scanning from side to side. But Mallory claimed to see him carrying Bengali's body.

The recording was useless. Any normal person watching would see what Mallory saw, influenced by the magic that had corrupted the image.

I was going to have to find some other way to convince him of Palle's innocence.

"Stan, I know you believe what you're seeing but that's not what's on the DVD. It's been tampered with, magically."

He sat back in his chair, crossing his arms over his chest. I could almost hear his eyes roll in his head.

"Come on, Noel. I know he's your friend but the evidence is right there." He pointed at the screen.

I opened my mouth to respond but was interrupted by an officer poking her head in from around the door.

"Detective, we got a call for you," she said.

"Isn't there someone else on duty?" Mallory asked. "I've got a full plate."

"You'll want this, sir," she said. "It's related to the others."

Mallory sighed. "All right, send it through."

The phone on the desk began to buzz. Mallory pushed the glowing red button and picked up the receiver. "Yes."

The scowl on his face faded into a blank expression that he wore when he was trying to control himself.

"On my way," he barked after several moments then hung up the phone.

"Let's go," he said, getting up from his chair.

"Where?" I asked. "What happened?"

"Nadia Judges, Palle's lawyer, is dead."

CHAPTER

TEN

Despite the illustrious Bay Street address, the parking garage looked like every other parking garage I had ever seen. Grey concrete with round grey pillars. Bright yellow arrows pointed the way going in and exiting. Good thing since the route was anything but intuitive. I felt even the reindeer with their perfect sense of direction would get lost down here without the arrows pointing the way.

From what I could see, Mallory barely glanced at them as he barrelled along, driving lower and lower into the bowels of the parking garage.

I hung onto the passenger door handle breathing through my mouth to avoid the stale smell of old coffee and older food containers.

Finally Mallory screeched to a stop that jolted me against

my shoulder harness, surprised that the airbag hadn't deployed. By the time I'd untangled myself and pushed the door open, Mallory was already slamming his door shut.

The flat, omni-directional light that permeated the garage gave way to several spotlights blazing with the power of a thousand suns, or at least they felt strong enough to burn my retinas. Two of the spotlights pointed down at a spot behind a dark blue sedan parked three spots over.

Yellow police tape was strung across the area and as I crossed in front of Mallory's car I saw he'd stopped within an inch of the tape. He had already ducked underneath and was halfway toward the blue sedan.

I ducked under the tape and followed.

At least five police officers worked the scene, several on hands and knees, dusting the garage floor or swabbing at tiny drops. As I came up behind Mallory, I realized the tiny drops had grown large enough to show as blood dripped on the grey concrete.

Suddenly I didn't really want to see around him.

Too late. I was already here.

I glanced down at the grey concrete before I moved to the side. Stepping in evidence was not the way to endear myself to the officers. As I glanced at the ground, I noticed one of the officers crouching by the fender of the dark blue sedan. She wore latex gloves and had a small brush in her hand. She gave me an approving nod.

I took it I was safe to step to the side.

I did so, coming out from behind Mallory.

Nadia Judges was sprawled on her back, arms flung out to either side. Her legs curled under her, as if she was about to sit up. Her head was turned to the right, away from me so I didn't have to see her face. Her jacket was closed but looked sunken into her chest.

"How?" Mallory said.

Several of the officers looked at each other. Finally one stepped forward. He looked older than the others.

"That's just it, sir, the how is pretty weird."

"Show me," Mallory said.

"Yes sir." The officer crouched down beside the fallen woman. He took hold of the left lapel of her jacket. Blood smeared on his latex gloves. The jacket was saturated but the navy colour hid it.

He lifted the edge of the jacket and nodded down.

Mallory took another step and looked.

I didn't want to, I really didn't want to, but the weird was why I was here.

I swallowed the sour bile that rose in my throat and followed Mallory's lead. I peered down.

A ruined hole was where the woman's chest should be.

"We think he took her heart, sir," the officer said.

MALLORY SAID NOTHING AS HE LED ME AWAY FROM THE BODY. HE stopped three columns away from his car, far enough not to be overheard. He turned to me, still keeping his back to the crime scene.

"So, what can do that, Noel?" he asked. "Rip a heart out of a woman's chest?"

I shook my head. "I don't know. I mean I'm sure there are things that could do it. I'll have to look into it."

"What about your friend, Palle? Where was he last night?"

"Stan, you can't think he did this."

"Why not? Maybe he disagree with his lawyer. Wouldn't be the first perp to do that."

I shook my head. This was craziness.

"What's wrong with your hair and your beard?" Mallory asked.

I reached up to grab a piece and pull it toward my face where I could see it. The curl stretched out. Instead of a deep brown, it was fading. The tip was already white.

Damn the halls.

I turned to the closest car and bent down to look in the passenger door mirror. The colour was fading fast from my hair. My beard was already white.

The dye should have lasted longer than this. The only reason my hair and beard would turn white so quickly again would be in reaction to strong magic.

Like the kind that would rip a woman's heart from her chest.

I turned back to Mallory.

"Something magical killed that woman," I said. "That's the only reason my hair and beard would be turning white so fast."

"Um, why is it turning white in the first place?" Mallory asked.

I sighed. "Beside I'm Kris Kringle's son. It's part of the whole Santa Claus legacy."

Mallory frowned. "But I thought you weren't in line for that, your brother is."

"I'm not," I said. I wagged a piece of hair at him. "Tell my hair that."

"And it turning white makes you think this death was magical?"

"I know it is," I said. "That and how it looks like her heart exploded out of her chest. That doesn't happen very often."

The lingering frown on Mallory's face told me he wasn't totally convinced.

"I want you to bring Palle in anyway. I want to talk to him."

"Stan..."

"Just talk, that's all. For the moment. Will you do that or do I have to send someone after him?"

"I'll do it," I said. "But you're just going to talk to him, right?"

"Right."

"You promise?"

Mallory pressed his lips so tight together they almost disappeared.

"Okay." I held up my hands in surrender. "I'll do it. After I take care of this."

"Put on a hat," Mallory said. "You have him in my office in two hours or I'll get him myself."

He turned away and headed back toward the body. I ducked back under the police tape and walked away. I followed the green sign pointing out the pedestrian exit and found an elevator. It wasn't until the creaking door closed and the elevator started up that the acrid stench of blood faded from my nostrils.

Get a hat. I had a hat. I had several in fact, I just kept forgetting them in the office. Which meant I kept having to buy them. At this rate, by the end of winter, my entire waiting room would be filled with hats.

The elevator dinged and the door slid open. My senses were assaulted by a rush of activity. I found myself in front of a food court. People hurried back and forth, several carrying coffee or little bags of snacks. Others unbuttoning coats. A variety of aromas warred for my attention. Roasted coffee beans, Mexican tacos, Italian sauces, Chinese noodles.

For a moment the shock from the empty parking garage to a bustling food court stunned me. I glanced around at the wall where the elevator let me out. To the right was a sign for the PATH.

Of course, I understood now.

The PATH was an underground, indoor system that

connected various office buildings and even a subway station or two in the downtown core of the city. Someone had told me once that you could walk from Bloor Street all the way south to Front Street without exiting the underground system once. And that didn't include riding the subway.

I'd never managed to find my way through the entire length of the system but one thing it did have besides food courts were shops.

The kind of shops that would sell hats.

Although it was mid morning, people still walked through the area. Through the crowd I saw the sparkling twinkle of Christmas lights that had been wrapped around the counter that blocked the food court from the main walkway. Coloured tinsel in red and green spiralled up several columns. As I followed the crowd, I spotted plastic wreaths on the walls. Cut-outs of snowmen and Christmas trees.

Even the occasional Santa Claus in a sleigh with reindeer.

And I could feel people starting to look my way.

I had to get a hat. Fast.

So far I'd passed several women's clothing stores, a cigar store, a variety store, an office supply store, but no men's clothing store. I was just about to give up and check out the women's store when I spotted something ahead on the right. Randal's Men's Clothiers.

I ducked behind a woman in a dark purple dress who was just raising her arm to catch my attention. She had the faraway look of someone who loved Christmas.

Of course the Christmas stocking broach on her dress might have given me a clue.

But before she could speak, I darted through the glass door, into the shop.

Whew, close call.

"May I help you, sir?" said a deep voice behind me.

I turned.

The store clerk was tall and thin, wearing a discreet pin-stripe grey suit. It was so immaculate, not even the plastic green name tag spelling out BRENDON could ruin it. He looked to be in his late forties with thinning grey hair cropped close to his head. His ears were tiny but his angular nose made up for it. He seemed to bend over me and for a moment, I thought he was going to bop me in the head with his nose like that glass bird doll that tips forward with its beak as if to drink, then tips back.

"Um, I'm looking for a hat," I said. "Like a knit touque or beanie."

He raised a bushy black eyebrow. "We don't sell that kind of hat here." His head tilted as he seemed to regard me. "But I think we may have something more suitable."

He turned and waved me to follow him deeper into the shop.

I followed past several round tables of kerchiefs, ties with matching tie pins, cuff links, and other assorted gift-type items. Sprigs of holly and mistletoe decorated the tables. Around the edges of the tables hung silver tinsel.

Rows of jackets and dress pants lined the walls. Colours

ran from black all the way to a deep, rich emerald green and all shades of grey and blue in between. Toward the back I caught a glimpse of a shimmer. Was that a deep purple jacket?

Brendon the clerk angled toward the left corner. Tucked against the back wall was a narrow, shelving unit made from dark cherry wood. The shelves were full of hats. A round mirror with a gold metal base sat on the wood case beside it.

Brendon picked up a dark grey fedora hat.

"Let's see how this fits," he said. "I bet I got the size right. I'm very good at guessing head sizes."

"That's not quite what I'm looking for," I said. "I want something to make me look a little less..."

"Like Santa Claus?" he asked. "Trust me, this will help with that."

He handed me the hat. Up close I could see it wasn't just grey, it was more a tartan grey with some deep red mixed in.

I turned toward the mirror and put the hat on my head.

It rested right on top, not pulling down on the sides or back. Way too small.

So much for Brendon's size guessing ability.

I glanced over at him, raising an eyebrow.

"Hmm, I thought for sure that was the right size," he said.

"The brim is a little much," I said. "I'd prefer something smaller."

"I have just the thing." He plucked the hat from my head

and returned it to the shelf. After a few moments, he pulled out a black bowler hat and handed it to me.

"This is a little larger, see how that fits."

I turned back to the mirror and slid the hat onto my head. It slid all the way down and only stopped at the ridge of my eyebrows.

"A little too large," I said.

"I'll get it." Brendon managed to lift the hat off my head with a quick flick of his wrist. He returned it back to the shelf. He lifted and replaced several hats in quick succession. Finally he picked up another one, dark grey, with a small brim than the fedora but a larger ribbon around the middle part.

"Try this," he said. "It's a Stingy Brim."

I set it on my head and looked in the mirror. It fit properly. The dark grey blended well with the navy of my coat. And best of all, it hid most of my hair.

It also looked pretty stylish. It made me look like a successful private detective. I just had to live up to the hype of this hat.

Which meant stopping a killer.

I stared at myself in the mirror. Even with the slightly too bushy white beard, I looked serious, competent, determined. I looked like a man who could do what it took to stop these deaths, even if I didn't quite know where to start.

I turned to Brandon and gave him a nod.

"I'll take it."

After the initial price shock, I didn't pay attention as

Brendon rang up the sale. I stared at the row of suit jackets to the right of the counter. One good thing about being my own boss, I didn't have to wear a suit too often.

Brendon made a slight noise of surprise. "There's a fifty percent discount on that hat. Pre-Christmas sale." He smiled. "Merry Christmas to you."

I smiled back at him, then without thinking about it, I said. "Merry Christmas, Brendon."

His expression softened. His eyes got a faraway look to them. He tilted his head.

"You know, you really do look like…"

Swirling snow, I'd almost got away without revealing too much of myself.

I snatched my card out of the credit card machine, making sure to drop the machine down on the counter. It banged, startling him.

Brendon gave a shake of his head and blinked. Confusion crossed his face.

"I don't need a bag," I said. "I'll just wear it."

"Sure," he said. He tore the bill off the top of the cash register. "Here's your bill."

"Thanks for your help." I grabbed the paper and crumpled it into my pocket. Before he could say anything more, I turned and hurried out of the store.

If possible, the flow of people along the PATH was even denser than before. But this time, the hat did the trick. No one gave me so much as a glance.

Like the second security guard on the DVD.

I had no doubt that whatever security tapes that covered the parking garage would be as equally useless as the ones from the Bengali Foundation. Whoever, whatever, was killing these people knew how to cover their tracks, in the regular world and to magic users.

I was going to have to be smarter and better.

And I was going to need some help.

So why not start with someone who needed to help himself?

I headed for the subway and Palle.

ELEVEN

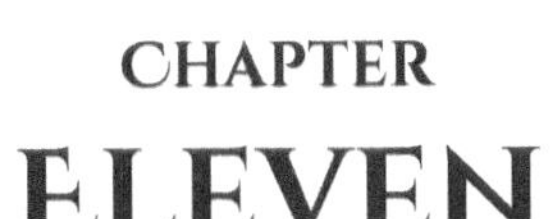

Palle didn't answer the buzzer at his apartment building.

The sky was overcast, creating a dull greyness to midday, but someone had slung a line of Christmas lights along the front of the old warehouse where Palle had his loft. At first I thought they were twinkling but then realized the sputtering of the light was from some fault in the wires. The flickering was too irregular to be one purpose.

I tried the intercom again, pressing the button on the beige keypad. The ringing sounded tiny and forlorn in the cold air.

And remained unanswered.

I felt a tightening in my chest that had nothing to do with the cold.

Where was Palle?

I couldn't imagine that he had killed Nadia Judges. She'd been trying to help him. But I also had to remember that he was a troll and therefore his actions weren't bound by being human.

Except the only time I'd seen him ever be violent was under the control of an evil entity. On his own, Palle was gentle and kind. One of the last people I would ever suspect of hurting anyone on purpose.

So where was he?

Not here obviously and standing around as the snow slowly soaked into the bottom of my pants wasn't going to help. Besides, I still had to find a way to replace the Toy Stash, get KJ his runners for the sleigh, apologize to Venir, and find out what creature that second security guard really was. That was the real answer.

And when I'd forced Mallory to see beyond the illusion on the DVD, he mentioned it had been wearing red robes.

I pursed my lips. I didn't know what that was but I was going to find out. In the meantime, I needed to trim my beard and colour it and my hair.

Again.

WHEN I *WINKED* BACK TO MY OFFICE, THE FIRST THING I NOTICED was the rich smell of percolating coffee, wafting in from the waiting room.

As usual, I landed in my office chair. It squeaked under me as I stood up to take off my navy coat. I hung it on the nail on the inside of my office door then unwound my red scarf from my neck. It tucked nicely on the nail as well. When I tried to place the hat on top, it slid off onto the floor.

I scooped it up. Well, that wouldn't work. I set it on my desk, beside the green desk lamp. Now it really looked like a stereotypical private detective's desk.

I chuckled to myself as I stepped through the doorway into the waiting room.

Palle perched on one of the yellow plastic chairs. His human façade had fallen away. In the yellowish, overhead light, his light green skin looked an even darker green. The large tusks that grew out of either side of his mouth gleamed. He held a tiny coffee cup in his massive hand that made him look like a grown up playing tea party with a child.

The short, four foot ex-Christmas Elf sitting beside him only made the illusion stronger.

Venir pressed his lips tight together as he lifted his chin. He wore jeans stuffed into cowboy boots that hung a foot from the floor as he sat in the chair beside Palle. A scuffed, black leather jacket lay on the chair beside him. He wore a grey flannel shirt with the sleeves rolled up to the elbows. His white hair curled up on his head, barely covering the tops of his pointed ears.

I tasted sour regret at the sight of him.

"Want a cup of coffee?" Palle asked.

"Ahh."

He took my bare stutter for ascent and set his own cup down on a leather coaster on the old, wood coffee table in front of him. The coasters were embossed with SC Private Investigations, a present from Venir at my one year anniversary. I almost winced at the sight of it.

Palle stood up from the chair. The plastic gave a groan as if relieved he was gone. One step and he was at the coffee maker, busying himself with fixing me a cup.

Venir just glared at me, pressing his lips tighter together. A muscle jumped along his jaw line.

I wanted to say something to him but no words would come.

So I turned to Palle.

The troll was just pouring my coffee. I waited until he had set the glass container down before I spoke.

"Palle, where have you been the last few hours?" I asked.

He paused after pouring in milk. He straightened and his bald head just about brushed the ceiling.

"I was at home and then came here, Noel," he said. "Why do you ask?"

I resisted glancing at Venir. "There's been another murder. It was Nadia Judges. Your lawyer."

Palle's left hand squeezed reflexively. Milk shot out of the top of the carton, reaching almost to the ceiling before splashing to the floor. I heard a clump as Venir's boots hit the tile.

"You don't think I did it, do you, Noel?" Palle asked.

"Of course I don't," I said. "But this is the second death associated to you. Mallory wants you to come in."

"You don't go nowhere," Venir said.

I glanced down. The Elf was pointing at Palle. His other hand had closed into a fist.

"You can't be trusting humans," Venir said. "They'll stick it to ya every time."

"Venir...," I said.

The Elf jerk his head toward me. His green eyes seemed to blaze in anger.

"Not even you," he snapped.

"I cannot believe that," Palle said. "Noel has been trying to help me since this began. And he saved me from the spirit. I owe him my allegiance."

"Well I don't," Venir said.

I opened my mouth to respond but he vanished. The spilled milk trickled into the spot as if drawn by his sudden disappearance.

"Are they sure she is dead?" Palle said.

For a moment I didn't know who he was talking about then I blinked and the memory of the hole in Nadia Judges' chest came flooding back.

"Yes, they're sure," I said. "Her heart exploded out of her chest."

Palle frowned, his tusks jutting toward either side of his face.

"Can humans do that with their hearts?"

"No they can't," I said. "It was definitely magic. Just like Troy's death was." Another memory rose up, this time of the DVD and the second security guard.

"Palle, do you remember seeing a second security guard at the front desk?"

He nodded. "A young man."

"Yes," I said. "Do you remember him leaving the desk, coming over to talk to you, and then taking the elevator upstairs?"

Palle tilted his head. He looked just beyond me as if envisioning the scene. I studied him carefully and saw the same drifting off as I'd seen in Mallory's expression.

"I don't remember that," the troll said.

"It happened," I said. "It's on the security surveillance but Mallory can't see it. There's definitely been a spell cast and I think you were caught up in it too."

"If that is true, why do they think I did it?" he asked.

"People don't believe magic is real," I said. "Only a few people like Mallory and Shirl know about it. If too many found out it could destroy their society. We have to find a way to deal with this ourselves. But first we have to find out who did it."

"But if Mallory knows about magic, can he not help me?" Palle asked.

"He's a police detective, he has to follow the law. And

this spell affected him too, so much that when I tried to get him to see beyond it it almost sent him into a coma."

I described it for Palle. With each word, the troll's frown deepened.

"All red?" he asked.

"That's what he said. I didn't even see that."

"It could be part of the magic, part of the spell to stay hidden."

"Do you know who uses such spells?" I asked.

The troll shrugged. "There are so many who use objects in their spell casting. I would have to investigate."

In order for him to investigate, he would have to remain free. Which would mean I couldn't bring him to Mallory, despite Mallory's request. Defying the detective was more than just ignoring his request, it was breaking the law. But I knew Palle couldn't have killed Nadia Judges. He didn't have the ability to do the magic that had killed her.

Of course Mallory might be understanding.

And we might get a massive heat wave for Christmas, melting all the snow and turning the city into a tropical paradise, all in the next half hour.

"Go investigate," I said. "Only come back when you find something. Not before then. If you do, I'll have to take you to Mallory."

Palle froze. He was so still it was like he had turned to stone. After a moment, he blinked.

"Will you not get in trouble for this?" he asked.

"Don't worry about it. You need to go now. The sooner

you can find me something the sooner I can clear your name."

He opened his mouth to speak again, then closed it again. He nodded.

"Thank you for your belief in me, Noel."

Before I could respond, he began to murmur under his breath. He set the coffee cup and crumbled milk carton down beside the coffee maker then made strange symbols in the air.

The temperature in the room dropped. I felt the little hairs on the back of my neck stand up. Goose pimples prickled on my arms. The smell of ozone curdled my nostrils.

Then I heard a deep rumble that seemed to come from the air in front of Palle. His image shimmered, reminding me of heated air rising from the asphalt in summer but that didn't match with the coldness in the room.

For a moment, Palle stood frozen. Then he took a step forward.

And disappeared.

The shimmering in the air vanished. The temperature began to level out and the ozone smell faded from the air.

Was that the troll version of a *wink*? Somehow I didn't think so. I didn't think he was travelling to any other place in this realm anyway.

"Good hunting," I whispered. Then noticed the pool of milk still spreading on the floor.

The least he could have done was clean up before he left.

I sighed and crossed to the bathroom for a towel to wipe up the mess.

THE COFFEE WAS STILL SOMEWHAT HOT BY THE TIME I FINISHED wiping up the spilled milk. I carried my cup and the wet towel into the bathroom. I rinsed the towel out in the bathroom sink and noticed my curling, solid white hair gleaming back at me.

Burnt coals, here I went again.

I squeezed out the towel and hung it over the back of the toilet. I took a gulp of coffee, noticing there was too much milk in it. Once it got down a little, I could top up the cup with more coffee.

Who needed to sleep tonight anyway?

I turned back to the mirror. It was the front part of an old metal medicine cabinet that usually held only a lone bottle of Aspirin but when I opened it up, boxes of hair colour were neatly stacked on the three shelves. They were all the various types and shades that Venir had found to replace the one I'd liked that had been discontinued.

Last time I'd had to colour my hair, he'd been here to help me.

I sighed and picked up a box on the bottom shelf. The picture made the brown look a little darker than my usual colour but maybe that would last a little longer against the white.

Fat chance.

I closed the cabinet and set the box down on the side of the sink. Before I could colour, I would have to tame this mess. I picked up the scissors that sat in the cup alongside my toothbrush. Grabbing a piece of hair, I stretched it out and snipped it off.

Snip snip snip.

I didn't bother trying for any kind of style. This time I had to be brutal. Soon the sink was full of my curls, then I used the scissors to trim my beard the same way. When I was done, I glanced in the mirror. My hair was barely two inches long. My beard trimmed right to my face.

Neither would last at this length, I knew. As Christmas got closer, my hair and beard would continue to grow, continue to turn white. I was fighting a losing battle with that magic but I had to keep going if I wanted to do any work on this case.

And I had to, for Troy's sake and for Palle. And for the other innocent people who had been killed and would be.

Because I had no illusions. Whoever this was wasn't done yet. I could tell. I didn't know how, it was a feeling. There was something about these murders. They weren't just regular killings. There was a deeper purpose. They had the feeling of ritual.

The strong stench of hair colour made my eyes water. I blinked rapidly, trying to stop the tears from streaming down my face as I continued to rub the brown mixture into my hair.

That was it. A ritual. These weren't murders just for the sake of murder, they were doing something else. Something powerful and something truly horrendous. Only the darkest, nastiest blood magic would use murder like this. Most blood magic required only a few drops of the caster's blood. But someone was doing some heavy duty magic and that someone was pretty heavy duty themselves. Not only were they doing this ritual, but the magic to hide it was enormous.

My mouth tasted sour, and it wasn't just from the hair dye.

What had I gotten myself involved in? Did I even have the ability to stop it?

The hair dye bottle burbled. A blob squelched up from the top. I was squeezing the plastic. I forced myself to loosen my grip. My head was covered in hair dye. Now I just had to wait for it to work.

A distant ringing sounded from my office. Damn the halls, my phone. I glanced at myself in the mirror. My hair stuck out all over, covered in hair dye. The tips of my ears were covered in brown. I grabbed some toilet paper and wiped them off. My skin looked just a shade darker than normal.

But holding a phone to my ear would squish dye into it and into the receiver.

Maybe I could at least see who it was.

I made sure the towel draped over my shoulders was securely tied before I hurried out to my office. Just as I reached the door, the phone gave a final ring and stopped. I grabbed the set and swung it toward me.

Too late. The display was empty.

Whoever it was would leave a voicemail if it was important.

Besides, I had quite enough on my plate at the moment.

I had no idea how buried my plate was going to get.

CHAPTER

TWELVE

Hair dye seems to take forever to rinse out but the water finally ran clear. I turned off the taps in the sink and used the towel to rub my hair dry. When I lifted the towel off my head, brown hair stuck up around my scalp.

Good. Hopefully that would last a few days.

I hung the towel to dry and carried my cold coffee back into my office. As I sat down, I set the cup beside the phone.

The phone was dark. No voice mail light blinked.

Whoever had called hadn't left a message.

But maybe the indicator wasn't working properly. I dialled in for messages.

Nothing.

I frowned. Who would have called me?

I tried to dial back but it dead ended. Phone number unlisted.

Strange.

I sipped the coffee and grimaced at the cold, bitter flavour. Even only half drunk, I could feel the caffeine coursing through my veins. I would be awake for hours now. Might as well try to do some work.

I fired up my laptop and input all the names of victims. Billy Wattle, Suzanne Delson, Troy Bengali, Nadia Judges. All prominent Toronto citizens, all dead within the last week.

How many others might have died that the police weren't aware of?

I opened the search engine program that Shirl had built for me. It wasn't quite as good as having her search for me but it was better than I could do on my own. She had mentioned that she had spiders crawling the web, gathering data. All I could picture was millions of tiny, black spiders scurrying around.

I didn't need to know more.

I entered everything I could think of: the names, their jobs, their community status, and let the program go to work.

While it chugged away, I slid my notebook across the desk blotter and flipped it open. The pages seemed to crackle with magical energy. I jotted down my thoughts about the case so far, the names, the strange presence from the other day.

If I'd hoped for any insights while I was writing, none came.

Then I made a note about the toy stash.

I had to find a way to replace those toys or to get the toy stash out of evidence. I couldn't let Troy's legacy be ruined and I couldn't let those families down. There had to be a way.

My mind stayed stubbornly blank. The only thing that rose up was worry about Venir.

Somehow I had trespassed on something painful to him. It had to be why he left the North Pole. Why KJ didn't like him. I'd never pressed Venir about it. It wasn't my place. It was his business. But now I'd hurt him out of ignorance and I wanted to find a way to make it up to him.

But how could I when I didn't know what the issue was?

The laptop pinged. Finished.

I turned toward the computer.

A list of eight names filled the screen. I sucked in a breath. How could so many other prominent people die and the police not be aware of it?

I started clicking through.

The first, Melody Treadmire, a clothing store heiress had died in a drowning accident in the Caribbean. Not such a shock except that she had once been in contention for a spot on the Olympic swim team.

Then Graham Wellington, owner of several car lots, who died of a heart attack on the way out of his doctor's office. After receiving a clean bill of health.

Third and fourth were twins, Dennis and Derek Fassell who ran a veterinary clinic for wounded wild life. They died in a single-car accident. In the early evening, on a bare street, and neither had alcohol on their breath. But there was a dead crow at the scene.

Sameer Jahanni, owner of several popular Indian restaurants, had died of cancer. Although he'd never been diagnosed with it.

Sara and Jerry Collins, owners of a real estate conglomerate and patrons of the opera, found dead of asphyxiation in their home, in the same room as a carbon monoxide detector.

And finally, Jensen Carmichael, an up-and-coming artist who had just completed a successful show in a small gallery on Queen Street but was scheduled for larger shows in the new year. He had died of a severe allergic reaction, despite having no allergies.

That made twelve prominent or famous people dead within the last few weeks.

Burning coals, what was going on?

I copied the list down in my notebook.

Was there some connection between them? Did they donate to the same charity, belong to the same groups? Maybe share the same accountant?

I wasn't sure Shirl's search program would be able to figure that out but I set the parameters anyway and plugged in all the names. As it ran, I spun in my chair to face the window. The springs squeaked in protest.

Outside it was snowing again. Fluffy gentle flakes drifted down from the sky. The parking lot outside my window was a vast black hole of darkness. One anemic light lit up the far right corner, casting a pale yellow circle that seemed to penetrate only a couple of feet, highlighting mounds of snow. The parking lot was rarely used and never plowed. With this snowfall, no one would use the lot until spring. Even the distant warehouses were mere suggestions of mounds in the darkness.

Out there somewhere some creature was stalking the city, using powerful magic to kill. And not just kill, but to draw to itself even greater magic.

What was its end game? And how many more would have to die to complete it?

If I knew one answer, I could probably figure out the other.

The problem was getting that one answer, and I had to do it fast, before someone else died.

Twelve deaths were already twelve too many.

Behind me, my computer chirped. I swung back around to see what the program had found.

Nothing helpful.

Five of them donated regularly to the same hospital. Four used the same accounting firm. Seven had subscriptions to the ballet. Five to the opera. Four were patrons of the zoo.

Although several activities and donations overlapped, there wasn't one thing that all of them belonged to or all of them did.

So much for finding any link between them. The only thing they all had in common was their prominence in the community, and being dead of course.

Wait. Prominence.

Was that the link?

It seemed rather tenuous but I couldn't see anything else that linked them, nothing else they all had in common.

Ring the bells, I'd go with that for now, until a better idea occurred to me.

I made more notes in my notebook. After a minute, I noticed that the lines on the page were wavering. My jaw cracked as I yawned. The caffeine that had been coursing through my veins, jolting me awake seemed to have burned out. I could feel my shoulders sagging.

Time to go home.

I turned off the computer, snapping the lid shut. I stood up from the desk and stretched. The stiffness in my back tightened and then released. I picked up my new hat and plunked it on top of my head.

As I wrapped my scarf around my neck and slid my coat up my arms, I considered my couch. I *could* sleep on it and I had on occasion. But if I stayed here, Mallory would probably be busting down my door first thing in the morning, looking for Palle and demanding to know why I hadn't brought him in. If I headed to my apartment for the night I might just be able to avoid the detective while I continued my own investigation.

I couldn't very well tell Mallory about it in-depth, not

and risk him having another seizure. No matter how much I wished I could ask Stan for help, I was not going to risk his health. I didn't think he was prominent enough to make the list but who knew what destruction this creature was capable of. I wasn't going to make Mallory a target.

I locked the door and headed for the stairs.

As usual, the alarm on the stairwell door to the outside was broken. It appeared to have a cycle of life that almost but not quite mirrored the year. In the spring, the building management became more zealous about security, perhaps in an effort to get more tenants. They would then install a new alarm on the stairwell door. But since the elevator was slower than a melting glacier, some tenant in the building would break the alarm so we could use the stairs without any hassle.

(Not me, it was never me.)

Over the intervening summer months, the building maintenance would try to repair the alarm but it would never work right and be continuously sabotaged, until any efforts at repair were abandoned in the fall. By winter, only a narrow pathway through the snow led tenants to the stairwell door, with mounds of snow and ice acting as more of a barrier than any alarm.

Then as the snows melted, the building maintenance would awaken from their winter slumber, surge forth with renewed enthusiasm and install a new alarm.

And the circle of life, and alarm vandalism, would repeat itself.

Working or not, the alarm never had any consequence for me. With a slight effort from my magic, I set it to ignore me the way it would ignore a slight change in airflow.

I was barely a disturbance.

As I turned the corner on the final landing heading to the ground, I noticed the last bulb had burned out, plunging the bottom of the stairwell into a thick gloom. I sighed. Behind me, the closest bulb gave out a weak yellowish glow. It was no more than forty watts, the cheapest bulbs the building could get. How long would they leave this last burnt out bulb in before they changed it?

Maybe as a Christmas present to the residents I should do something about that.

I lifted my hands, ready to weave a spell, when I cause a slight whiff of ozone.

A lingering scent from the bulb's final hoorah?

No, I shouldn't have been able to smell that. This had a distinct odour. One I was intimately familiar with.

The after effect of a spell.

Maybe that burnt out bulb had had a little help with the burning out.

Kind of like the one in my office.

I paused on the second step down and waited.

In the stillness, all I could hear was the pounding of my heart sending blood rushing past my ears. I took deep breaths, trying to calm my heart and my jagged nerves. It felt like the caffeine had returned with a vengeance, sending a surge of anxiety through my system. I remembered the feeling of menace from before, the burning cold.

But now I felt.

Nothing.

From the gloom at the bottom of the stairwell, I felt nothing. Emptiness. A staleness in the air from the stairwell being shut too long. With little direct access to fresh air, it always smelled a little stale in here.

Now it smelled exactly like that. Exactly like it always did.

Which only made me more suspicious.

I took another deep breath and started down the stairs again. I set each foot down deliberately, making sure I had steady footing before moving on. I held my hands out in front of me, moving them in a slight pattern. A small repelling spell, nothing to trigger any magical backlash that might be down there, but just enough to create a slight wedge. Enough that I could slip through.

My coat felt thick around me. I could feel sweat dampen my armpits and the base of my back. The scarf felt hot around my neck. My hat slid down on my forehead. The edge of it pressed just above the bridge of my nose.

Another step.

I couldn't see the stairs below me. I reached out to my right and felt the wall. The paint felt gritty under my fingers. Dust.

Another step.

The darkness felt total, like I had gone suddenly blind. I could still feel the wall on my right but it felt like it was curving away. Another inch and I would lose track of it.

I felt forward with my left boot.

No further steps. I was at the bottom. I breathed in. The slight ozone scent was gone. Just the usual stuffiness.

Maybe the bulb *had* burned out on its own.

Sure.

And my hair and beard would stay brown for the rest of December.

Holding my hands out in front of me, I took a big step forward. My palms hit the bar across the door. It depressed against my forward momentum. The door creaked as it opened.

Cold, crisp air rushed in as if to embrace me. A slight, feeble light from the single street light in the corner seemed to shine with sudden brilliance after the intense black.

I sighed with relief as I stepped out into the night air.

Snow crunched under my boots as I followed the path out into the parking lot. The few tenants who did drive and park here stuck close to the back of the building. They burrowed their path from their cars to the stairwell and the rest of us followed along.

I had just reached the first empty spot when the parking lot light went out.

Cold air slammed down like a curtain. My muscles felt like they were seizing up. Around me the air crackled like ice.

Like magic.

Burnt coals, they'd waited until I let my guard down.

I could feel menace worming through the cold like slivers. This time it didn't seem to come from any one direction but all around me. I tried to turn my head but my neck felt like it was going to snap in the cold. My coat felt like a block of ice hanging off my shoulders, squeezing against my torso, making it hard to breathe.

The hat on my head pressed solid against my ears. The entire thing was frozen and brittle.

And I'd just bought it!

The flare of anger warmed me, pressed against the menace that was building all around me. I tried to discern where they were coming from. I had a feeling it was important, but the feeling was jumbled together. The threads had woven a web of threat around me and were tightening it like a noose.

A noose I might not be able to slip.

My heart pounded, sending useless adrenaline coursing through my body. My muscles tried to jump and move but all they could do was tremble against the cold.

I couldn't fight my way out of this, I was going to have to think.

But with the cold pressing tight against me, even that was getting more and more difficult to do.

I'd fought my way through this before, remembering my childhood at the North Pole, how I was so used to cold. But this seemed colder than I'd ever experienced. A cold that sank through my skin, through my muscles, even through my bones.

How could I beat a cold this deep? I felt like I was at the bottom of a pit and I couldn't even lift a hand to try to climb out. I felt my eyelids start to droop. It wouldn't make any difference if I closed my eyes. It was too dark for me to see anything anyway.

I let them close.

The pit deepened. The walls around me grew higher and higher. But they weren't smooth. Things jutted out from the walls, nooks and holes where I could put my hands and feet if only I could lift them.

But why would I want to do that? It was such a far way to go.

Better to just stay down here. Maybe even sit down.

I flopped and my movement stirred the air around me. It swirled against the wall in front of me, brushing dirt away from part of the wall. A part that jutted out near my face.

It was red and sparkly.

Beside it was something green and gold.

And just above it, was something round. Covered in blue with a silver ribbon.

Presents. Wrapped presents.

Christmas presents.

The kind my dad delivered every Christmas. The kind I needed to replace the Toy Stash.

Burning coals, I'd almost let go!

I had to reach for one present. The red sparkly one. It was

a rectangle, jutting out near my face. I felt my hands jerking as I forced them up. My fingers were almost as red as the wrapping paper. I could barely feel it when I tightened them around the crinkling paper.

Christmas paper. Christmas gift.

A thought tickled the back of my brain. Sluggish and slow.

Some way to push through the menace that still thickened around me.

I pulled on the present. It was stuck fast. My hands felt like they were frozen to it now.

Good. It might just work.

I leaned back, falling like a felled Christmas tree. The box resisted. Then slid forward.

And popped out.

A rumble sounded. Around me, the walls of the pit began to tremble. Dirt shook free, revealing piles of Christmas presents. The brightly coloured walls shivered and began to fall.

They piled around my outstretched legs. I managed to jerk my torso up as a cascade rushed down, pressing at my back. They held me up in a sitting position. But that was only tenable for a moment.

The walls rumbled around me as more and more presents began to fall. They covered my legs. Buried me to my waist. Then the flood of presents rose higher.

And higher.

I was going to be buried in presents.

Even with the weight on my legs, I could feel my muscles warming. I flexed my knees and my legs bent an inch. I was thawing out even as I was being buried.

Which was the better death?

Neither as far as I was concerned.

I still held the present in my hands. I pulled it closer to me. There was a card on top but the writing was blurry. I blinked trying to read it. Moisture dripped onto my face, into my eyes.

My hat was melting. I lifted my hand, trying to push it back on my head. I lost my grip on the package. It fell away, disappearing under the avalanche of presents that now pressed against my chin.

Who's present was it?

I felt the question ripple through my mind and the sluggishness fell away. I sucked in a deep breath and pushed out again.

What is your favourite Christmas present?

The frigid cold snapped away, leaving only the regular cold behind. Blazing yellow burned my eyes, making them water. My hands felt cold and wet. My body quivered with cold.

I was kneeling on the ground, my bare hands down in the snow of the path before me. Dull shadows stretched around me, weakened by the meagre light from parking lot light.

No presents. No menace. No freezing, death-cold.

Just fluffy white flakes drifting from the sky. And me kneeling in the snow, shivering.

Close. Too close.

This time it wasn't a warning. This time whatever it was had meant to kill me.

And it didn't matter that I wasn't prominent at all.

I now had a target on my back.

CHAPTER

THIRTEEN

S hivering, I managed to push myself up to my feet. Before I could consider going back up to my office I closed my eyes and *winked.*

I landed in the living room of my apartment.

It was a new place. I'd lived here less than six months but had managed to anchor a *wink* here. It was a nice one bedroom apartment on the top floor of a three storey house. The land lady, Mrs. Pealers, who lived on the main floor, loved the idea of a private detective living in her house. As long as I didn't shoot anyone on the property.

I had assured her that would not happen.

I opened my eyes. Pale light from the street lights outside illuminated the two narrow windows in the living room. I was standing on the chocolate area rug I had bought at Ikea, dripping melting snow on it and on the parquet flooring.

I could almost see the steam rising from my soaked clothes. The warmth on my face only made me more aware of how cold I was.

In two steps, I sloshed over to the front door to the right of the windows. I shrugged off my navy coat. It dripped on the rubber mat when I went to hang it up. I should probably hang it over the tub.

Something I would do after a long, hot shower.

I pulled the hat off my head. It now had the shape of my head, not the proper hat shape. I tried to squish it back into place. Water dribbled over my fingers. I set it on the baseboards near the door. Hopefully it could be salvaged.

Next I kicked off my boots before I sloshed my way through the darkened living room. I passed the taupe leather sofa that faced the windows. The surface glistened in the dim lighting.

Past the living room was the kitchen on the right then the hallway that led first to the bathroom, again on the right with the bedroom opposite it on the left. My stomach grumbled as I slipped past the kitchen.

First things first. I needed a hot shower and fresh clothes.

I peeled my clothes off and stepped into the old claw foot tub. When I'd moved in, Mrs. Pealers had apologized for the old tub and the circular shower curtain ringing it. It was old and somewhat water stained and she'd been meaning to replace it but hadn't had the time. I'd assured her it was all right, and it was. It reminded me of our claw foot tubs at home at the North Pole.

But now my muscles felt so cold I had to sit on the edge and lift one leg at a time into the tub, using my hands to help my leg muscles. I yanked the curtain closed and turned on the hot water.

Steam filled the room. I breathed it in, feeling the pounding water soak into my skin. My muscles felt like they were melting. Just before the water scalded me, I added some cold to get it a reasonable temperature.

I tipped my head back, letting the water run over my head and face. My muscles tingled and although fatigue tugged at me, I could feel my brain starting to work again.

Christmas, something about Christmas and presents sent whatever it was scurrying for the hills. Were they afraid to tell me what their favourite presents were?

Or were they afraid it would revel them to me?

That had to be it. Something about their favourite Christmas present would tell me who they were, and I knew it was a *they*, not just one thing. The multiple threads of menace told me that. Each had felt slightly different, although somewhat similar.

Like they were family.

Some kind of evil family that was killing prominent people in Toronto.

But why?

I shook my head, sending water droplets splashing on the plastic curtain. They trailed brown down the white curtain.

Oh no.

I yanked the taps off. The shower dribbled a final few drops before stopping. I squeezed water from my hair and watched it hit the bottom of the tub.

Brown. All brown.

Damn the halls.

Dripping, I climbed out of the tub and faced myself in the mirror. Steam covered the surface, making me a smudged blur. Please let that be a smudged blur with brown hair.

Please.

I snatched a white Christmas hand towel from the rack beside the sink and wiped the mirror down. Streaks filmed the mirror and then faded, revealing my face.

Complete with white beard and white hair plastered to my head.

My hands tightened on the edge of the sink until it felt like I was going to snap it off.

It was one thing to try to kill me, now they had not only ruined the one decent hat I had, they were messing with my hair colour as well.

Enough was enough.

I couldn't keep dealing with my hair and beard while trying to identify and stop these creatures.

So I did what I should have done at the beginning of December.

I opened the medicine cabinet and pulled out the hair clippers.

IT TOOK LESS THAN HALF AN HOUR TO REMOVE MY BEARD AND THEN shave off all my hair. With every soggy slap of hair hitting the sink I felt freer than I had in a long time. By the time I finished, the steam had evaporated from the bathroom.

I stared at myself in the mirror and saw a stranger.

I'd never not had a beard, not since I hit puberty. A full head of facial hair was one of the Santa Claus legacies. Usually I managed to keep it trimmed fairly close to my face but at Christmas, it went crazy.

And my bald head...

I ran a hand over my scalp. I could still feel a shadow of hair. I turned my head to the left and right, checking it out. It was... different.

But I had no illusions. This was a temporary solution. If I was lucky, I'd get a day out of it, maybe two, before white locks cascaded to my shoulders and a white bushy beard covered my chin.

But for now, it was one less thing to worry about.

I turned away from the mirror and headed out of the bathroom. As I hit the light switch, it felt like a switch had turned off in my body. Fatigue pressed down on me.

I stumbled across the darkened hall into my bedroom where I flopped onto the bed. Within seconds, I sank into sleep.

My eyes felt crusty when I opened them. Pale, grayish light filtered through the blinds on my left. Strange, the light should have been coming from behind me.

Then I realized I wasn't asleep on the couch in my office, I'd actually made it home.

My body ached as I crawled out of the queen-sized bed. I felt like an old man as I moved through my morning ritual. My face in the mirror startled me when I splashed water onto it. The shaving was still in place. Mostly. I could already see some stubble on my bald head.

I dressed in my grey suit and even added a burgundy tie. By the time I headed into the kitchen to make coffee, I was starting to feel human again.

Unlike at the office, I didn't have a Keurig in the small, galley kitchen. I used a plain drip coffee maker that sat just to the left of the white stove. Although there was ample cupboards in the kitchen, the counter space was negligible with the stove on one end and the fridge at the other end right by the door. The sink bisected the space in the middle, leaving only two slivers of space on either side. Just enough for a coffee maker on one sliver and the toaster on the other.

I carried coffee and toast into the living room and sat down on my taupe sofa. The leather sank beneath me, soft and luxurious. I'd found it on sale at Ikea along with the rug.

A slight imperfection on the left arm had gotten me a large discount.

As I sipped coffee and nibbled at my toast, my mind began to churn.

Christmas, it all came down to Christmas. But Christmas was a time of festivity and joy, not death and blood. What were these creatures hoping to gain by using their blood magic at this time? It had to be something big and they had to have some connection to Christmas otherwise why wreck such havoc at this time? If there was one thing I knew about magic, it was that conjuring such power was very much dependent on timing. Magical beings that had an affinity for summer time weren't as powerful in the winter and vice versa. So it stood to reason that whoever was doing these killings and gathering this power was doing it now because they had to. They had some affinity to winter.

Some affinity to Christmas.

I just had to figure out who it was.

I finished my coffee and left the cup in the sink. As I brushed my teeth, I noticed the stubble on my chin. My beard was already try to reassert itself. I took a moment to shave again.

There. Maybe it would last to the end of the day.

My coat and scarf had dried overnight but both were stiff from the thorough soaking. I slipped them on as I stuffed my feet into my boots. Then it was time to check my new hat.

Setting it on the baseboard had dried it although it still hadn't returned fully to its original shape. I squeezed it, trying to get the proper indents for the fedora-type look. It held it well enough so I set it on my head.

There, now I was set to face the day's challenges. I only hoped I'd be able to solve a few of them.

By the time I reached my office, I could smell the rich scent of coffee seeping out from around the door jam. I opened the door.

Palle was hunched over the Keurig machine. As I closed the door, the troll turned, holding a coffee mug in his giant hand. He gave me a nod but no smile exposed his tusks any more than they were already.

Bad news then.

"No luck?" I asked.

"Nothing so far," he said. He stepped back from the coffee machine. One leg brushed one of the yellow, plastic chairs against the wall. It fell over with a thud.

Palle flinched. His heels thumped down on the floor. I imagined that it sounded like something breaking through the ceiling in the office below.

"Take it easy," I said. "Just relax, Palle."

The troll shifted the mug from one hand to another. He was nervous, I realized.

"What is it?" I asked. "What's wrong?"

"Are you going to take me in to Mallory?" he blurted out.

Ah, that was it. I'd told Palle to only come back when he found something, otherwise I would have to take him in to the police.

But that had been before the attack last night. Before I realized it was a gang of creatures.

I was going to need all the help I could get.

I shrugged off my coat and carried it into my office.

"I'm not going to take you in," I said. I took off my hat and set it on my desk, then I stepped back into the waiting room.

"I need your help to stop whoever is doing this," I said.

"Noel, what happened?"

Shock made the troll's mouth drop open, exposing his tusks. His hands were loosening. I noticed the cup slipping in his left hand.

"Palle, your coffee!"

"What? Oh yes." He tightened his grip but not too much. The cup didn't shattered, but I did notice a slight shake in his hands.

"I shaved," I said. "Everything. Every time there's a slight hint of magic around me, my hair and beard turn white. I'm spending a fortune on hair dye and not getting any benefit." I ran my left hand over my scalp and felt a solid buzz of hair brush my palm. "At least this way I maybe have a day or two of reprieve. I need it to stop the creatures who are doing this."

Palle tilted his head. "Creatures?"

"I was attacked last night," I said. "It was more than one presence. Definitely."

I described the attack and my own vision of the presents that helped me block and ultimately dissolve the attack. By the time I finished, Palle was nodding.

"This does change my own inquiries," he said. "I agree they are tuned to winter and Christmas. But I cannot guess at their final objective."

"Neither can I," I said. "I just don't want any more people killed."

"What do we do next?"

He looked at me with such expectation, like I would know what to do.

Too bad I didn't.

I would have to fake it.

I considered the list of victims. Standing in front of the Toy Stash in the lobby of the Bengali Foundation, I hadn't felt even a trace of magic. Whoever had cast the spell had done so with perfection. But had they been that perfect at every scene, especially the first few? Maybe between the two of us, we could find something.

"We're going to check out the scene of the first murder," I said. "But first I want a coffee."

CHAPTER

FOURTEEN

Fortified by coffee and with my list firmly in hand, Palle and I *winked* to the first scene.

The side road where twin brothers Dennis and Derek Fassell had died was a quiet, residential street. The section where they had swerved off the road was bordered by an empty park on one side and a row of three bungalows on the other.

Palle and I landed on the sidewalk in front of the park. The snow lay like an unbroken blanket across the ground. A few bare trees poked up, their branches crusted with snow. In the centre of the park I spotted a set of swings, empty of the swinging part, and a set of monkey bars. They looked like skeletons of some ancient animals.

Salt crunched under our boots as I led Palle a few paces to the concrete pole that the brothers had crashed in to, losing their lives. From here, even with the snow piled along the road, the surface of the street looked bare. Not even a hint of ice. There could have been ice at the time, even black ice, I knew, but I had a feeling it wasn't ice that had made the brothers crash.

I considered what I knew about them. Dennis and Derek had grown up in Scarborough, developing a love of animals passed down from their mother as they grew in a household full of pets. They both went to veterinarian school and after finishing, they volunteered to work overseas. That was were they had gained fame, rescuing animals in war zones and disaster areas. Often times performing makeshift surgery and managing to reunite many pets with their owners. After five years of such work, they had returned to Toronto to start up their own practice, with half the profits going to a charity they had helped start to continue their work for animals in underprivileged areas.

Their photogenic looks: wavy, black hair over ruggedly handsome faces and deep blue eyes, as well as their compassionate devotion to animals, had made them the darlings of morning television shows and in-demand at their clinic. The wait-time to get an appointment had grown to six months.

Then one evening, as Dennis drove his brother Derek home from work, they had swerved on this empty street and slammed into this concrete pole, dying on impact.

No trace of the accident was visible even though it had only happened a few weeks ago. Instead, a pile of frozen floral bouquets and wilting cards were scattered in the snow at the base of the concrete pole.

I stopped at the pole, looking down at the soggy, frozen tributes. The air was crisp and cold, carrying that freshness that only seemed to come from frozen temperatures. But I couldn't feel anything else. No hint, no spark of magic.

Was I wrong? Had this actually be an accident?

Had I conjured up this entire thing in my head?

Maybe these early 'victims' weren't victims at all.

I turned to ask Palle if he felt anything.

The curtains in the window of the middle house across the street shifted.

Someone was watching us. Fortunately, Palle was in the habit of holding onto his human form outdoors. Still, even that form was pretty imposing.

I held up my hand to him. "Wait here a minute."

My boots tapped hard on the bare asphalt as I hurried across the street. I climbed over the snow pile on the other side. The sidewalk and the paths to all three houses were cleared off. I headed up the centre path.

The bungalow was light brown with butter yellow shutters. The front door was a darker brown with a small round window in the top. It was frosted with the image of a bird carved into it.

I rang the doorbell. The chime rang out loud then faded to nothing.

No sound came from behind the door. I waited. I was sure I'd seen the curtain move.

Still nothing.

I lifted my hand to press the doorbell again when the door yanked open. An old man who would have been taller than me if he wasn't hunched over glared at me. Wisps of white hair curled on the top of his ears. His skin was a pale, waxy colour, showing a lack of sunshine. Deep lines creased his forehead and around his mouth. His light blue eyes held a glint of steel in them.

"Wadaya want?" he demanded.

"I was just wondering if you knew anything about the accident a couple of weeks ago," I said.

"You a reporter?" he asked. "We don't like reporters."

"I'm no reporter, sir," I said. "I'm a private detective."

I pulled out the silver card case Venir had given me last summer. Seeing it made me almost wince. Would I ever get a chance to make it right with him?

I couldn't focus on that now. I had to keep on track.

I pulled out one of my cards and passed it over to the old man.

He frowned as he moved the card up and down in front of him. He tilted his head back and then forward again. Finally he scowled.

"Too damn small ta read," he said. "Margie, where's my glasses?"

He yelled this last bit back through the door behind him.

"In the kitchen, you old coot," came a yelled reply.

A flash of expression crossed the old man's face. He jabbed a finger at me.

"You wait here."

Then he stepped back, and the door slammed in my face.

I waited. I'd been ready to dismiss him as a crotchety old man until he'd reacted to the old woman's voice that answered him. No matter how fast he'd tried to hide it, the smile that had lit him up lingered in my mind. There was magic in a smile like that.

A couple of minutes later, the door opened again but instead of the old man, it was an old woman. Dressed in a pale blue dress, her feet stuffed into overlarge, fluffy bunny slippers, she smiled at me. Her skin was the warm brown of rich leather. Her black afro was frosted with white.

"You a private detective with that name?" she asked. A chuckle hinted at the edges of her voice.

"I am, ma'm," I said.

"You come in for tea then."

She held the door for me. I stepped past her, into the house. Pale peach wallpaper with delicate flowers covered the wall that led into the living room. A darker peach sofa sat facing the front windows. Above it was a collage of photos in silver frames. From the foyer, I could only see the largest of them, images of the couple when they were young, smiling and happy.

I stood on the rubber mat while the old woman shuffled past me. She stopped in front of me.

"I'm Ronda Marshall," she said. "You've met my husband, Will."

"Yes," I said. "I just wanted to ask a couple of questions about the accident outside."

"Terrible thing," she said. "Just terrible. Brothers and veterinarians. People who like animals are good people."

I nodded. "Did you see the accident?"

She turned and started shuffling past me, waving me to follow.

"Such a shame," she said. "Come in the kitchen for tea. Don't worry about your boots, it's all tile this way."

She led me past the edge of the living room, down a narrow hall that ended at the kitchen. Inside, the peach motif had been replaced with pale yellow and dark blue backsplash. A dark blue Formica table sat just to the right of the doorway. The old man Will sat at the far end. He scowled when I walked in.

"Feedin' him now, are ya?" he said to Ronda.

"You stop," she said. "Drink your tea."

He stirred a spoon in his cup. "I want milk."

"You can't have it. You're lactose intolerant," she said. "Wait for the next shop."

He grumbled again but I could see the edges of his mouth turn up. This was a familiar game for them.

Ronda busied herself at the counter. When she turned back, she held two mugs of tea. I stepped forward to take them from her but she shook her head. I settled for pulling out the old chrome and vinyl chair for her. She smiled her thanks as she set the cups down on the table.

"Have a sit," she said as she settled down.

What could I do? I sat.

The tea was hot and strong. The flavour burst in my mouth, sending a jolt through me. I set the cup back down.

"The accident…" I said.

"Yep, damn shame. Loud bang. Weirdest thing ever," the old man said.

"Why weird?" I asked.

"Didn't hear no screeching tires," he said. "They drove straight inta the pole."

"Will…" Ronda said.

"They did," he insisted. "I heard it. No screech at all. Like they was aimin' for that pole. Hit it right on, they did." He gulped his tea.

"After the sound, did you see anything?"

"Ya mean did I get up to gawk?" he said.

I lifted my cup to avoid answering.

The old man grunted.

"Tell him," Ronda said.

The old man gave a great sigh, as if this was a huge burden he had to undertake. Ronda kept a straight face although I could see the shadow of a smile at the edges of her mouth. She hid it by lifting her own cup.

"Okay, yeah, I got up ta look. Anybody would."

"Anyone would," I agreed. "What did you see?"

"The car all busted up," he said. "Terrible. All I's could see was the back end but it looked too short. Could tell the front end was smashed up cuz of how it looked truncated." He shook his head. "Had my phone in my hand calling nine-one-one faster 'n nobody's business. Called it in even though that other guy probably called in too. But I never wants to assume."

He took another sip of tea.

"Another guy?" I asked.

"Yeah," Will said. "By the driver's side window. I figgered he was seein' if he could help. Nice thought but too late, I imagine."

I'd not read anything about someone near the car at the time of the accident.

"Can you tell me about this guy?" I asked. I sipped my tea, trying to stay casual.

"Couldn't see 'im too well," the old man said. "Was dark and all. Well past sundown. I don't think he was wearing a coat which is crazy in this weather. Looked like his clothes were all flapping around 'im, like rags."

"He wouldn't be wearing rags," Ronda said.

"Didn't say he was," Will said. "Just sayin' it looked all flappy like rags."

"Anything else?" I asked.

He frowned. His eyebrows drew together, deepening the lines in his forehead. Finally he shook his head.

"Nope. Don't think so."

It wasn't enough. I needed more to go on, more than just a figure in rags. Was there a way to coax more out of the old man?

I took another sip of tea and focused on him. It took barely a moment for me to learn that his favourite Christmas gift was a train set his father had given him when he was seven. His second favourite gift was the pocket watch his wife had given him three years ago. He still carried it in his pocket even though he spent most of his days in this house within a quick glance of multiple wall clocks.

As I focused on him, I saw the lines around his eyes soften. His shoulders drooped a little farther.

"Ronda, you get my phone? There might be some pictures there."

For a moment, I thought she was going to good-naturedly tell him to get it himself but something in his face made her nod her head. She pushed herself up from the table.

"E'scuse me," she said.

When she left the room, the old man started talking again.

"Thought something strange about 'im leaning in the window," he said. "Look like he stretched all the way in, like a rubber man. Kinda the way I always thought Santa would be comin' down the chimney."

A dreamy look settled onto his face. My influence was shifting his focus toward Christmas. I had to get him back on track.

"What else can you tell me about the figure?" I asked. "Could you see his face?"

"Naw, just the ragged clothes, all red and kinda dripping. Splattered on his boots some. They was black with white fluff on the top."

"The top?"

"Yeah, around the top edges. Went about halfway up the calf. Good boots for stompin' around a train yard."

The sound of shuffling feet sounded behind me. Ronda entered the room. She set a smart phone down beside the old man's cup.

"You find it," she said. "I don't know your password."

"Ha, it's the date of our first," he said. His brows wagged on his forehead.

Ronda gave a mock gasp. She slapped his arm. "Will, you old dog."

He chortled as his fingers flitted over the smart phone. A moment later, he was scrolling down on the screen. Finally he stopped.

"Here ya go. I snapped a shot when I thought the cops might wanna talk to 'em." He frowned. "I forgot to mention him to 'em."

"He probably didn't see anything," I said.

Will extended his hand with the smart phone. I motioned for him to put it down on the table. My magic had a bad habit of messing up smart phone technology. It was the reason I could only use a flip phone as a mobile.

I bent over the table, peering at the screen. The image was fuzzy, unfocused, but I could see the back end of the car clear.

At the driver's side...

A figure in red hunched over the window, just like Will had said. I couldn't see it's head as it was hidden by the angle of the car. But the boots did look black with white fur trim around the top.

Like some bastardized Santa Claus look.

Who or what was this thing? Why were they doing this?

I leaned back in my chair and lifted the tea cup for another sip. It was cold.

"Anything else you can remember about that night?" I asked. "Anything strange or different?"

The old man shook his head. "Nope. That crash was strange enough."

Ronda sipped her tea. "There was the Christmas carols."

"Carols?" I asked.

"I didn't hear nothing," Will said.

"You wouldn't, you old coot," Ronda said. A smile flittered across her mouth. "You're deaf as a post."

The old man brought a trembling hand up to his ear. "Eh? What's that?" Then he leaned toward her. His hand moved below the table. A moment later, Ronda jumped and gave a sharp laugh.

"You stop. We've got company."

"You heard carols," I said, trying to bring them back onto topic.

Ronda shook her finger at Will and then turned back to me. "Yes, it was quiet, soft, but it seemed to come from all around me. At first I thought it was only in my head but then there was the crash and it stopped."

"What was the song?"

"Santa Claus is Coming to Town," she said.

I felt a chill run down my back. I set the cold cup of tea down.

"Thanks for all your help," I said as I got up from the table.

Ronda smiled. "Our pleasure, son. Happy to help. You come on by any time."

"Well, not just any time," the old man grumbled.

"Will!" she said.

"What?"

I left them to their playful bickering as I closed the door and stepped back out into the cold.

CHAPTER

FIFTEEN

When I stepped out of the house, Palle waved at me from across the street. The sky had turned a sleet grey, dulling the sun light. Snow crunched under my boots as I crossed the street to reach him.

"The accident was definitely magically induced," I said. "The witnesses in that house said they didn't even hear any tires screeching. Just the crash, like they drove right into the pole. Before it happened, the wife heard a Christmas song and afterward, the husband saw a figure leaning down into the car. A figure dressed in red with black boots."

Palle frowned. "What does it mean, Noel?"

"I don't know." I sighed and looked back at the pole. I wished Venir was here. Being as connected to Christmas as I was, he might have had some insight into who or what the figure was. Palle, while eager to help, didn't have the same background.

I needed someone to ease my creeping suspicion. It could *not* be my dad. There was no way. In the first place, he was far too busy right now to be involved in anything outside the North Pole.

It had to be something trying to look like him. Or something connected to it in some way.

But who? What?

And for what purpose? What possible reason could there be to kill these people? Assuming there even was a reason.

The concrete pole didn't have a scratch on it. No indication that such a short time ago, it had been involved in a fatal collision. There should have been a mark. The passing of two men in such a violent and sudden fashion should have left something behind. But I could see nothing in the smooth, greyish surface of the concrete pole.

In one motion, I yanked off my glove and touched the pole.

The surface was cold, the sharp, crisp cold of stone. Then I felt the texture, both smooth and pebbly at the same time, scratchy against my palm. As I ran my hand down the pole, there was still no indication of a dent. Just the smooth, cold surface.

Everything went dark.

I blinked. It wasn't pitch black. I could see lights from the houses across the street. I turned my head to the left. The park was a dark blob. The sky above was a deep, slate grey, just before turning to full night.

But it was the morning.

I took a deep breath but couldn't smell anything.

I wasn't here. It was a vision. Some kind of magical residue.

The concrete pole didn't have any visible damage but it had held onto something from that night.

Something had left a mark on the pole after all.

I became aware of the hum of an engine in the distance. Pin pricks of headlights appeared, growing to large blobs of light as they grew nearer. The engine rumbled louder, tires crunching on new snow. The rumble grew into a roar. The headlights blazed forth powerful beams that sliced through the darkness.

I could almost make out the shape of the hood and the expanse of the windshield.

The engine revved higher. Ice popped and cracked like gun shots under the spinning tires. The headlights yanked toward me.

And grew into supernovas as the car slammed into me.

I was a shadow, an illusion, even as I tried to jerk away. I felt nothing as the front end of the car smashed into the concrete pole at my side. The shriek of metal filled my ears, then silence as even the roar of the engine died, leaving only the tingle of crumbling glass.

In the sudden darkness, the shattered windshield was like a dark spider web. I thought I saw movement inside. The shift of a head against a headrest. The flutter of a hand reaching for the window.

I tried to move toward them even though I knew this was only a recording. These men were already dead. There was nothing I could do to help them.

Then I felt a deeper cold pressing against my right arm. It tingled for a moment and then my arm went numb.

From the darkness, a figure glided forward. It seemed faded, almost transparent, like an old photograph that had been sitting out in the sun too long, bleaching out all colours. As it moved closer with a smoothness that made it appear to hover over the ground, I noticed the red of its coat. Faded and pale, but still red. A red hood hid the figure's face from view.

Hands with long skeletal fingers, pale skin stretched so tight it looked like it would peel away at the knuckles, protruded from the sleeves of the red coat. Matted, off white fur covered the cuffs of the sleeves and lined the bottom of the coat. It hung long, stopping just above the black boots, which were also cuffed with matted, off white fur.

It looked like someone's evil version of a Santa costume.

And it pissed me right off.

I could feel my anger start to burn, masking my fear.

As I watched, the hands lifted. The pale fingers touched the driver's side window, then passed through it as if it wasn't even there. They settled around the top of the door, gripping the edge. The figure leaned forward. The hood dipped down as it leaned through the window.

"Leave him alone!" I shouted even though it was useless. This was only a recording. A memory. Nothing more.

Then the figure turned its head toward me.

Damn the halls.

It had to be an illusion. It had to be. I wasn't at the crash site. I was standing beside the pole, touching it, weeks after the fact. I stood where the left front headlight would have been. Even if I *had* been there, I would have been crushed in the crash.

The figure couldn't possibly see me.

Could it?

But even as I denied it, I could see the figure turn. The hood tilted as if it was considering me. Then it slowly began to pull out through the window. The hands released the car door. The figure began to turn.

Toward me.

Burning coals!

It couldn't affect me, it couldn't touch me. But no matter how many time I told myself that, fear coursed through me. The figure took one step and then another. With the crushed front end, I stood only a few feet away. Another few steps and it would reach me.

I didn't want my heart ripped from my chest.

I yanked my hand from the pole and jumped back. My boots tangled together. The right one slipped on the ice and I fell on my rump.

Brightness blazed forth.

"Noel, are you all right?"

Palle knelt beside me. Weak sunlight filled the sky, brightening the neighbourhood around us. The street in front of me was empty of the wreckage I had seen just a moment ago.

I sucked in a lungful of the cold, crisp air and let Palle help me to my feet.

"Did you see anything?" I asked him. "Hear anything?"

The troll shook his head. "You put your hand on the pole and closed your eyes. A moment later you fell down." He frowned. "Are you sure you are all right, Noel?"

"Yeah, sure," I said. My legs felt only slightly wobbly. Another deep breath steadied them, and my resolve.

"I'm going to head back to the office," I said. "Call me in a few hours to check in."

"I should come with you," Palle said.

"You can't. You're a fugitive now, Palle."

His shoulders slumped. He nodded. "I remember."

"Don't worry, I'm going to figure out who did this and who framed you," I said. "I want you to stay hidden until then."

"I do not like leaving you to deal with this alone," Palle said. "There is magic involved. I could feel it coming off you when you were touching the pole. Without Venir..." He stopped and looked down.

I'd thought I'd kept my wincing under control. From the way Palle looked away from me, maybe I hadn't.

"I can handle it," I said. "If you came with me, you'd

probably end up arrested and in jail. This way, you're still free to help me if I need it."

"Of course I will, Noel," he said.

I smiled. "I know, Palle. Now get going."

I followed him as he walked to the corner and turned toward the park. Just a few feet in was a large oak. The trunk looked frosted with cold. It was so thick that when Palle ducked around it, he was hidden from view.

I waited a moment, then followed his path, kicking and dragging my boots to smear the trail.

As I expected, Palle was gone. He'd *winked* to parts unknown. I hoped it wouldn't be for long.

I took a glance around, making sure I was out of view of any gaze, then *winked* myself.

My desk phone was ringing when I landed in my chair. I yanked my hat off my head and tossed it onto the desk before I grabbed then receiver.

"SC Investigations," I said.

"Kringle, where you been?"

Shirl Trombley's voice practically crackled over the phone line. It was almost as bracing as a cold splash of water.

"Working a case," I said. "Just a second."

"Kringle..."

The growl of her voice faded as I set the receiver down on my desk blotter.

I stripped my coat off and hung it on the nail on the back of my door. Since I couldn't fit a coat rack in here, the nail had to do, but maybe I could spring for a hook.

Some day.

I hung my scarf over my coat and turned back to the desk, running a hand over my scalp. Instead of the bare stubble, my fingers combed through several inches of hair. I wasn't going to look but I bet it was white.

Sitting back in my desk chair, I picked up the receiver again.

"Hi Shirl, sorry about that," I said. "Have you found the sleigh runners?"

"Still lookin'," she said. "Gotta couple of leads. Should know in a couple days. But that ain't why I called."

"Oh?" I said. I flipped open my notebook and made a note about the sleigh runners. A couple of days, say Wednesday then. Maybe Thursday at the latest. If I could get them that quickly, I'd make sure Shirl got an extra large bonus tacked on to the bill.

"No, it ain't. I had another reason." I could hear her puff out a breath over the phone line.

"What other reason?" I asked.

"Okay," she said. "What the hell is goin' on with you and Venir?"

"Venir? Is he over at your place?"

"Not at the moment," she said. "I sent him out for bagels. Get him outta my hair. What I wanna know is why ain't he in yours? He's driving me nuts."

"We had...a misunderstanding," I said.

"Misunderstanding," she said. "He said you insulted him."

"I didn't," I said. "I asked him if he could look after getting toys to replace the Toy Stash that was confiscated."

"Confiscated? Why were toys confiscated?"

"Never mind that," I said. "He got upset and left. I think it has something to do with why he left the North Pole but I don't know the exact reason. Did he tell you?"

She sighed. "You think this is some kinda soup opera? I don't know why he's pissed at you, he just keeps ranting. If you want those sleigh runners, or anything else ever, you're gonna come over here and make it right. Got it?"

"Got it," I said. "On my way."

But she'd already hung up in my ear.

I smoothed my tie down as I stood up. It felt like it was going to be a day where I would forever wonder why I both- ered to take off my coat. At least I had a hat to cover my hair. I stuck it on my head and got ready to leave for Shirl's place.

BATHURST STREET WAS A MIX OF WHITE FLUFFY SNOW AND brownish, messy slush. The white fluffy snow clung to the edges of the buildings or piled between them. The slush took over everywhere else, mostly at the street corners where it dissolved into slushy puddles.

I waddled through one puddle as I crossed the street toward Shirl's brownstone apartment building. The normal carefully tended front yard was covered in a thick mound of snow, most of it white with a spray of brown thrown up by the passing cars. But the walk was well shovelled and salted as I hurried up the path to the door.

Shirl answered on my first buzz. The door clicked open. I grabbed the handle and slipped inside.

Shirl lived on the top floor, the last apartment down the hall from the elevator. As my boots squished along the thin carpeting toward her door, it creaked open and Shirl stuck her head out. She pointed at the black plastic mat beside the door.

"Boots here," she said.

I obliged. I kicked off my boots, leaving them dripping on the mat before entering her apartment in my socks.

The living room looked the same as always. Piles of boxes covered the walls, filled with electronic parts. I was never sure, but they seemed to change over time, different ones taking the place of older, sagging pieces. In the middle of the space, was Shirl's large, curved desk covered with three large monitors. Her blue leather chair was tucked in.

I turned to Shirl. As usual, she wore her hair in long, thin, braids piled high on her head to give her the illusion of height although she barely came up to the top of my chest. She was wearing a dark forest green pullover sweater with a Christmas tree knit onto the front of it. It was long enough that it covered the thighs of her black jeans and if she hadn't pushed them up her arms, I was sure the sleeves would have dangled past her hands. Her feet were covered in her favourite hightop red sneakers.

She glared at me as I walked in.

"Bout time you got here," she said.

After the vision, I hadn't wanted to use up my meagre magic so had to resort to the streetcar and subway. I'd still managed to get here in under an hour. Super speedy considering the weather.

"Where's Venir?" I asked.

"I sent him out to the store for cream cheese. Don't want plain bagels." She closed the door behind me and crossed to her chair. She flopped down into it then pointed at a tall, chrome and leather bar stool covered with two boxes.

"Sit," she said.

I knew better than to refuse.

I shifted the boxes to the floor and dragged the stool out a little before sinking down onto the leather. It had a tiny back that supported me better than I expected.

I loosened my scarf and unbuttoned my coat before taking off my hat. As I did so, Shirl's eyes widened, the whites shining against her black skin.

"What happened to your hair?" she practically shouted in astonishment.

"I shaved it all off," I said.

She shook her head. "No, the colour."

I sighed. "It's white, isn't it?"

She nodded. "You look just like…"

I held up a hand. "Don't say it. I know." I ran my hand over my head and felt the luscious growth. It felt like it was almost as long as I usually kept it.

So much for shaving helping it last longer.

"I'm here about Venir," I said.

"Right, right." She shook herself. The childlike wonder dissolved from her face as she settled back into her usual look of mild disdain.

"You are gonna settle up with him," she said. "He'll be back any minute and I want him outta my hair and back into yours."

"I know," I said. "I've already apologized and I willing to do so again. I just wish he would talk to me about it."

"He'll talk. I'll make sure of it."

I couldn't say anything to that. I gestured at her sweater. "Nice."

Her eyes narrowed. "You makin' fun?"

"No, of course not."

After a moment, she nodded, satisfied. "My gran made it for my brother, but he's too cool to wear it."

"He wasn't too cool for Dinosaur Bones Play Set," I said.

A startled look came over her face. "How'd you do that? You ain't never met him."

I shook my head, spreading my hands. "It's a Christmas thing. I'm more sensitive than ever at this time of year and you were there when he opened it."

"Okay, fine," she said. "But don't tell me about anybody else."

I was about to agree when the door clicked open. Before I could stop myself, I swivelled around in the stool.

Venir stood in the doorway, one hand on the doorknob, the other clutching a plastic bag. He wore his boy's parka open on a plain, brown, cable knit sweater. A blue knit cap was pulled over his ears. White curls puffed out from underneath.

His eyes widened at the sight of me and his lips thinned. His chest puffed up as he took a deep breath, preparing to *wink* away.

And ruin any chance we had of working it out.

CHAPTER

SIXTEEN

"Don't you move!"

Shirl's sharp command sliced through the air between us. Venir's gaze shifted off me. The stomp of Shirl's shoes sounded as she stormed past me.

She reached the door and pulled it farther open, yanking it from Venir's hand. She pointed into the living room.

"Get in here."

A muscle along Venir's jaw jumped as he clenched his teeth. His hand tightened on the plastic bag, making it crinkle. The sound crackled in the silence.

"Venir, you know I hate repeatin' myself," Shirl said.

The ex-Christmas Elf threw a bit of his glare her way, but only a bit. He didn't want to incur her wrath any more than I did. Shirl had an unsettling way of making even the strongest of us hesitate.

Venir took a step inside as he released the door. It brushed his parka as it closed.

Shirl was already on the move. She swooped down and grabbed the plastic bag from Venir's hand as she passed, heading for the kitchen. As she reached the doorway, she called back.

"I'll be toastin' up bagels for a snack while you two *talk*."

I could tell from her emphasis on that final word that neither of us would be allowed to leave her apartment if we didn't comply fully with her instructions.

I extended my hand toward her chair.

Venir frowned, looking even more sour, but he moved deeper into the living room. He slid past me and over to Shirl's desk chair. When he sat, I noticed his feet still touched the floor, barely. He kept his parka on, tugging it tight around his waist. His head bowed so he didn't have to look at me.

Any apology tasted sour in my mouth. He'd already rejected my previous attempts to apologize. I had no illusion I'd have any success this time with that strategy. I was going to have to try another tact.

"I could really use you on this case," I said. "There's been ten deaths so far of prominent figures in Toronto and the only clue I have is that magic is involved and there's a figure in a red, fur-trimmed coat and fur-trimmed black boots."

Venir looked up at me, frowning. But this time the frown was one of concentration, not displeasure.

"Red coat?" he asked.

I nodded. "Some of the deaths have been made to look like accidents or natural causes but I went to one of the scenes earlier today and the magical remnants pulled me back into it."

"Powerful," he said.

"Very," I said.

He stayed silent but I could tell he was thinking. Thinking about the case and not about how angry he was at me.

Small steps.

Even if I didn't know exactly what had happened, maybe we could still work together. Maybe eventually he would trust me enough to tell me. In the meantime, I would avoid that particular landmine by not asking anything about the North Pole.

I would find some other way to replace the confiscated toys.

But first things first.

"You see this red figure in the vision?" Venir asked.

"Yes," I said. "I couldn't see any face. It had its hood up and it was dark inside when it turned toward me."

The Elf jerked upright in the chair. His hands gripped his knees, forgetting all about holding the parka closed.

"It saw you?" he asked.

I felt my face turn warm. "Yes."

"In the vision?"

I wanted to look away in embarrassment but didn't. "Yes."

"You ijit," he snapped. "It's got yer scent now. How did it see you?"

"Well, I kind of yelled at it to stop."

He huffed out a breath and rolled his eyes. "Fer snow's sake, what are you doin' yellin' at it in a vision. If it left magical residue powerful enough to trigger a vision, don't you know it traces back to 'em?"

"I didn't know then," I said. "I do now."

He shook his head, mumbling under his breath so low that I couldn't make out the words.

"That's not all," I said. "Whoever it is has the ability to change technology enough to disguise themselves on security tapes as well as being able to hide themselves from Palle."

"How you know that?"

I described visiting Mallory at the station to view the DVDs of the security log. I mentioned how Mallory couldn't see the second security guard, even when I mentioned it and also the seizure that Mallory seemed to have.

Through my description, Venir's frown grew, the lines in his forehead deepened. He pulled his cap off his head and twisted the knit fabric in his hands.

"And he saw it in red too?" he asked.

I nodded. "Red coat like blood. I know it sounds like...well, like my dad but it isn't."

"No, it ain't," he said. "But it might be something close."

A chill tightened my shoulder blades. I forced myself to relax.

"What do you mean?" I asked.

"I can't be sure," he said. "I gotten check into it." He lifted his chin, looking me straight in the eye for the first time since he'd walked in the room. "If yer willing to work with me."

Silence filled the room, even the hum of the computer seemed hushed.

Here was where the water got choppy.

"I still think of you as one of the team," I said. "I'm not going to pry into your business but if I don't know something, I don't want to be blamed for my lack of knowledge. Can you work with that?"

His lips tightened, the skin turning almost as pale as his white, fluffy hair. Finally he puffed out a breath through his mouth. His shoulders drooped and his large, pointed ears bobbed as he nodded.

"Kay, I guess," he mumbled.

It felt like a temporary truce rather than a reprieve. I had a feeling we would be discussing this again.

Shirl poked her head out from the kitchen. The warm scent of toasted bagels drifted out around her.

"Now that everybody's friends again, what kind of cream cheese do you want? It seems that 'pick up some cream cheese' morphed into 'buy every kind in sight.'"

Venir straightened on the chair. "I didn't buy every kind. There were one or two I skipped."

Shirl snorted. "Sure, cuz they were the kind you didn't like. Right?"

A flush spread across Venir's cheeks. I pressed my lips together to stop a grin but it wasn't enough. Venir glanced at me and then glared.

"Hey at least my hair ain't white. Have you even bothered to colour it?"

"I have! Twice and then I shaved everything off."

"When?"

"Yesterday."

Shirl appeared in the doorway with a large butter knife in her hand. "You shaved your beard off yesterday?"

"That and my hair."

Her eyes boggled. "Yesterday? But it just looks like you got a trim. And bleached it white."

Venir tilted his head at me. "Went white after the vision?"

I nodded.

"I will have ta look into it."

"Later," Shirl said. "Now you're helping me eat these bagels and as much of this damn cream cheese as you can."

She waved us into the kitchen where she had a small table set up. The yeast scent of the bagels mingled with the rich scent of cream cheese. Seven tubs were opened on the table, each with their own knife sticking out. Shirl set a stack of toasted bagels piled on a plate on the table.

"Dig in," she said.

My stomach growled. After all the running around for the last few days, I couldn't remember the last time I'd had a full meal. Bagels and cream cheese wasn't exactly a full meal but it would have to do.

And as I took my first mouthwatering bite, I realized it would do just fine.

THE THREE OF US GORGED OUR WAY THROUGH TWO BAGS OF BAGELS. As Shirl opened up the third bag, I begged off.

"No more," I said. "I can feel my arteries hardening from all the cream cheese."

Shirl turned to Venir. "You?"

From the way the Elf smacked his lips I knew he was tempted, but he glanced over at me.

"Naw, gotta get back to work," he said.

Even with the gruff way he said it, I could see the edges of his mouth lift in the shadow of a smile.

Maybe we'd be all right after all. Even if there was this secret between us.

He'd tell me if he wanted to. I could live with that.

I picked up the paper napkin from my lap and wiped my hands.

"You'll call me when you hear about the sleigh runners?" I asked.

"Yeah," she said. "And just so you know, I'll be adding the cost of the cream cheese blow out to the bill."

Venir sat back, looking indignant, but I dropped my napkin on the table, drawing their attention.

"That's fine," I said. "Well worth it."

As I stood, Venir followed suit. We began to snap the lids back onto the plastic containers of cream cheese, plain, low fat, strawberry, chocolate, salmon, dill. Way too many and yet we'd managed to make a significant dent in them.

My stomach rolled a little looking at them. Maybe too much of a dent.

As I stacked two containers together and handed them to Shirl to put into the fridge, I caught her eye. She gave me a quick nod. Her gaze flicked to Venir and back to me, and added a smile to the mix.

I smiled back. It did feel like my team was pulling together again.

Then a ringing interrupted us.

"Your pants are ringing," Shirl said. "Is that your damn flip phone again? Why can't you get a normal one like regular folk?"

"A smart phone won't work for me," I said, as I pulled out my phone. "My magic screws it up."

I glanced at the screen.

Mallory.

Damn the halls. He was probably calling about Palle, how I hadn't brought him in yet. I would have to think of something to put him off.

I took a breath and opened the phone.

"Hello," I said.

"Noel, you have to help me," Mallory's voice was hushed and urgent over the line. "I think I'm losing my mind and I think someone's trying to kill me."

"Stan, where are you?" I said.

"Pine Ridge and...shit!"

The connection broke leaving me with dead air and a sinking feeling in my gut.

Prominent people. Stan Mallory had had several prominent cases over the past few years. I remembered teasing him about the articles in the Toronto Star. The framed copies his colleagues had foisted on him that he kept stacked on the side of his desk in his cubicle because he felt self-conscious about hanging them up.

Prominent...

Burnt coals.

"Whatever it is is after Stan," I said. "We have to stop it now!"

"How, kiddo, when we don't know what it is?" Venir asked.

I shook my head. Mallory was in danger. I had to help him.

"Where is he?" Shirl asked.

"He said Pine Ridge then he got cut off."

"Pine Ridge is north of Steeles," she said. "Ain't much up there, especially this time of year. Only thing is some tree farms." Dawning awareness brightened her face. "Christmas tree farms."

"That's it," I said. "Let's go."

"But..." Venir said.

"Come or not," I said. I shoved my arms into my coat, yanking it up onto my shoulders. I grabbed my hat and stuck it on my head. "I'm going."

Venir scrambled to gather his parka.

"I'll get the addresses," Shirl said. She ran out of the kitchen. Moments later she hurried back in, holding a single sheet of paper still warm from the laser printer. It had a list of four tree farm addresses. I showed it to Venir.

"First one, Pine Ridge Tree Farms," I said.

Venir nodded and we *winked.*

SNOW PUFFED UP AROUND MY SHINS AS I LANDED. THE AFTERNOON sky was overcast, darkening the day to twilight. I was standing on the side of a two lane, plowed road. Unfortunately, there was no sidewalk so I stood in a snow drift.

Trees and empty lots full of snow were the only things in either direction on either side of the road. I saw no sign of buildings, no houses. It felt like I was in the country even though I was in the northern end of the city and maybe only a block or two away from more urban sprawl. But here, it felt desolated and empty.

Five feet to my right I spotted a driveway and a large sign

with dark blue lettering in flowing script. Pine Ridge Tree Farms.

I climbed out of the drift and hurried along the road to the driveway. As I headed up, I spotted Venir standing in the centre of the drive. He had his back to me, the hood of his parka tucked down so I could see the band of white curls poking out from beneath his knit cap.

"Venir…" I called.

He spun at the sound of my voice.

"Nothin' here," he said. "I'm not detecting anything outta the ordinary."

"Are you sure?" I asked.

He nodded and waited for my instructions.

I looked down at the list. Venir was probably right. He would probably be able to detect the lingering effects of magic but what if it was so subtle he missed it? Were we hurrying off to check the next spot only to leave Mallory behind?

I was already wasting precious seconds worrying about this.

"Next one," I said.

We could swing back if we had to.

If I hadn't managed to screw up and got my friend killed.

No stress.

A moment later, Venir and I *winked* onto the driveway of the next listing, Choose Your Own Tree Farms. This time we landed farther down the drive, around a bend and out of sight of the main road. The air was hushed, sound muffled by the rows of snow-covered pine trees that lined the drive-way. They seemed to tower over our heads, pressing against the sides of the road. I'd never thought pine trees could be menacing but somehow these managed it.

In the silence and dim light, anything could be hiding in those trees. Just waiting for us to turn our backs...

I shook my head. I was letting my imagination get away from me. Focus on the task.

I turned to Venir. "Anything?"

He was frowning. From his pocket, he pulled out the stub of an unlit cigar and rolled it around his fingers. Finally, he shook his head.

"It's creepy here but ain't no magic."

Now it was my turn to frown. "Is the creepiness an indi-cation of something?"

"Maybe," he said. "But it ain't enough. There ain't no real trace here. You wanna get closer?"

I glanced down at the paper. Two more to go.

"Next one," I said. "Stapleson's Pines."

We *winked.*

Another driveway. More trees pressing against the sides of the road, blocking more light. It was enough to make my head pound, but I knew that wasn't the reason. Too many *winks* in fast succession for me. It sapped my meagre magic and gave me a magic-induced headache. The only thing to do was to rest and recover.

After Mallory was safe.

I turned to see Venir a few feet away. His back was to me.

I took a step toward him and noticed his left hand clutching the cigar butt.

Tight.

I took a deep breath, drawing in the cold air and the fresh, rich scent of the pine trees.

And the tickle of magic against my skin.

Here!

I stepped up to Venir's side. He glanced over at me. His face was pale, his lips pressed tight together. He nodded.

Definitely here.

"Can you tell what it is?" I asked.

He shook his head. "It's familiar but I'm not sure. I can't quite remember."

"Keep working on it," I said. "Meantime, let's go."

I stepped forward and felt him grab my arm, tugging on the sleeve of my coat.

"Wait a minute, kid, you just jumpin' in there? Without knowing anything?"

"Mallory's in there," I said. "He's my friend and I'm not going to let him get killed."

"You ever think this might just be a trap?" he said.

"Of course it's a trap," I said. "Think that's gonna stop me?"

Surprise flashed across his face then a grin settled on his features. It was his first real grin in a long time and nice to see.

"You're crazy, kid," he said.

"I know," I said. "Let's get Mallory."

We headed up the driveway. Snow crunched under our feet, loud and at the same time muffled in the still air. The line of trees seemed endless and after a minute or two, it felt like we were walking in place. The same trees seemed to pass by us, the same snow drifts. But the prickle of magic grew in my mind like an itch on my skin.

This was the place. It had to be. Although if it was a trap, the residue of magic gave it away.

Did they know that? Was that part of the trap or part of a fakeout?

Had I made a mistake thinking Mallory was here? Was I wasting time?

I picked up my pace, hurrying faster along the driveway. The ruts in the snow angled to the right as the driveway turned in a sweeping bend to the left. At least now I knew we were actually moving.

But not fast enough.

I had to get there faster.

"Kiddo, wait up!"

Venir's voice cried out from behind me but I couldn't wait. Not if I'd made a mistake. I had to know now so I could get to the next farm if I had to. I couldn't let Mallory down.

Around the bend, a wide, one-storey building came into view. Pale grey siding seemed to blend into the snow drifts, making the building look like some kind of winter mirage. Piles of snow were so high on the roof I couldn't tell it was peaked or flat. The path leading to the front door was matted from multiple steps but not shovelled.

The drive ran past the building and curved around to the right, behind it. Several snow-covered pine trees huddled at the corner of the curve, hiding the drive. I didn't see any cars.

How would Mallory have gotten here if not by car?

I wanted to head into the building, find someone and make them tell me what was going on, but the prickling of magic forced me to be cautious. As much as I wanted to, I couldn't just go barrelling in there, not without some ideas.

I stayed on the drive and followed it around the bend.

Past the trees, I spotted what was probably a parking lot during the summer. A long stretch of unbroken snow extended from the back of the building to my right about a hundred metres to the left and looked to be wide enough for two rows of cars.

One car was parked close to the back of the building. I recognized the blue of the sedan.

Mallory's car.

He was here.

As I turned to face the back of the building, Venir came huffing up to me. He pointed past me at the car.

"Is that...?"

"Yes," I said. "It's Stan's. He's here."

I could feel my hands tightening into fists. The prickling of magic made me as antsy as seeing Mallory's car. I was ready to bust in there.

Venir grabbed my sleeve.

"Kid, you don't know what's in there," he said. "You can't just go storming in there with no sense."

I yanked my sleeve out of his grip as I turned on him.

"So what are they? You seemed to think you recognized them. Can't you give me any idea, even if you aren't sure?"

"I don't know," he said. "It doesn't make any sense."

I wanted to grab him by the scruff of his parka and shake him. "What doesn't make sense?"

"If it is what I suspect, they would never do this. I don't understand." He shook his head.

"Say it or I'm going in."

He gave me a pained look, the same look he'd given me when I told him he couldn't smoke his cigar in my office.

"Fine, I'm going in." I turned toward the building.

And made it two steps.

"The Yule Lads," Venir said.

I turned back and stared at him. "Are you kidding me? The Yule Lads? They're just pranksters. These are no pranks. People are dead. Mallory's in trouble."

Venir's face scrunched up, deepening the lines around his mouth, his eyes, and across his forehead. He looked like someone had squished his face, between the top and his chin.

"They weren't always pranksters," he said. "Not until your dad took care of 'em."

"Took care of them?" I asked. "What do you mean?"

The Elf's hand flapped out. "Ya know, zapped 'em. Put the whammy on 'em. Made 'em see the error of their ways. They settled down after that. Got up to silly mischief, nothing serious. That's why it can't be them. They'd never go against your dad like that again."

"Are you sure?" I asked. "If they caused trouble before..."

"No way, uh unh, nobody goes against your dad a second time. You think he's all nice but he can be tough when he has to be. Dealing with anything that taints Christmas brings that out in him. No way the Yule Lads would cross him again."

Venir shook his head. He seemed so certain.

But if not them, then who?

I didn't have time to figure it out. Mallory was in there.

I took a step toward the door.

And stopped.

Mallory was in there. Wasn't he?

I pulled my phone out of my pocket and flipped it open. Even from the edge of the parking lot, residual magic itched on my skin like an irritant I couldn't scratch. It left me feeling agitated, restless, like I had to keep moving.

Reckless.

Or maybe that was what someone, or some thing, hoped.

I turned on my phone and checked the log.

My call with Shirl and then...

Nothing.

There had been no call from Mallory.

I felt a pop press against my ears, like the release of pressure after a long elevator ride. Venir gave a loud yell.

I spun.

The car was gone. Undisturbed snow showed it had never been there.

They'd fudged a security tape, faking a phone call should be no trouble at all.

It was a trap, and they hadn't even needed to use real bait.

"Venir, run!" I shouted before I felt a blast of heat from behind me and the world turned black.

CHAPTER

SEVENTEEN

The first thing I felt was a prickling heat against the back of my neck. It spread across my shoulders and down my arms to my hands.

Pulled back behind me.

After a moment, the prickling heat turned into a tingling of nerve-endings. My muscles and limbs aching and firing as they woke up and recovered from the magical blast. My eyes were still closed. I heard a faint humming sound.

I ventured a peek.

The darkness was not completely total. I could see the hulking shapes of things around me, hinting at a wider space. I was lying on my side on carpeting. The rough pile scratched my left cheek and it had the stale stench of being shut up for a while. Was I inside the one-storey building?

That seemed to be the only logical place. But I wasn't sure I was dealing with a logical situation.

Or a logical creature.

Could it be the Yule Lads? Would they have rebelled so strongly against my father? I couldn't imagine it. Sure, the Yule Lads may have been more blood-thirsty at one time but I couldn't imagine they'd do anything to disgrace Christmas. That had never been their way. They had staunching protected and enforced the rituals of Christmas. Killing these people in such horrible ways so close to Christmas, even putting the Toy Stash into jeopardy, wasn't something I could see them doing.

So if not them, then who?

And why?

I wanted to know but I wasn't sure I wanted such an up-close and personal experience of it.

I started to move my arms. The rough texture of rope scraped against my wrists. I couldn't detect any magic in them. Shifting my legs, I felt rope around my ankles. I was well trussed up but with some time I might be able to do something about it.

If I got that time.

I started twisting my wrists, seeing how much give was in the rope. My breath huffed against the carpet. Dust tickled my nose. I tried to turn my face away to get away from the stale smell but that shifted my hands into the carpet. When I lifted my hands away, my face mashed into the carpet.

Which did I prefer, breathing or freedom?

I prepared to breathe dust.

I was able to bend my right wrist so my fingers brushed the rope. Another moment and I felt the bulge of the knot. I dug my index finger into it. There was a smidge of space, a slight give.

As I worked on it, my eyes became more accustomed to the dark. The blob across from me to the right was a tall counter. To the left was a row of chairs. But I didn't see any people.

It was December. On a tree farm. Where were the people?

The rope tightened on my left wrist but I could worm a finger into the knot. Just a little longer...

The air prickled with static electricity. A moment later, the telltale tingle of magic danced on my skin.

Damn the halls.

It felt stronger than before, stronger even than outside my office. And like before, it tried to use cold against me.

Maybe it couldn't use anything else.

My teeth started to chatter. My muscles clenched with cold. My fingers started to go numb. It was hard to move them against the rope. All I'd needed was just another minute.

The feeling of menace flowed out from the space between the counter and the chairs. I stared through the gloom at the dark space. Something was there. Some one...

The red was so dark it was almost black. The hood hung

low, hiding its face in a shadow almost as dark as the darkness around it.

Hiding. Was it afraid I would recognize it?

In the cold, my mouth felt as parched as ice. I swallowed, trying to drum up some saliva. I coughed to clear my throat then I managed to lift my face an inch off the carpet.

"Who are you?"

My voice came out as a deep croak. The effort of lifting my head made my neck ache. I let my face drop down again.

No movement from the figure in the red coat. No sound either. The feeling of menace grew, flowing in waves, like a rolling swirl of snow. Chilling me to the bone. My flesh felt crusted by ice.

But if they were going to kill me like this, why tie me up? Their magic was enough to overwhelm me. They'd done it before.

But I'd escaped every time.

Maybe tying me up was a way to stop me from escaping this final time.

I grunted as I forced my shoulders to shift. My left arm ached as it pressed harder against the rough texture of the carpet. My fingers ached from the cold. Even my scalp ached. My hat had fallen off. Through lids crusted with ice, I could see the form of it lying a few inches away.

I'd barely had a chance to wear that hat, my own Christmas present to myself.

Christmas... It was about Christmas with these creatures.

Groaning, I lifted my head again. The figure in red blurred in front of me.

"Come clozzer," I slurred. "Waz your favourite Christmas prezent?"

The figure jerked. Its head reared back away from me.

The freezing cold around me lessened. I wiggled my fingers as blood flowed back into them.

"Tell me." My voice came out stronger as my vocal cords warmed up. "What is your favourite Christmas present?"

The figure shuddered. A low moan sounded from within its dark robe.

"Who are you?" I demanded. "Are you the Yule Lads?"

The arms flew up. Hands so thin they looked skeletal crooked into claws. It rushed toward me.

A flood of freezing cold bowled me over. I slammed onto my back.

The figure rose above me. The skeletal fingers grabbed my shoulders, nails digging in through my coat. They sent tendrils of frigidness through my muscles.

The figure wrenched me up as it shoved its hood down, facing me with darkness.

This was it. This was how I would die.

"Help... me..."

The voice was a low groan, as if torn from a ragged throat.

Wait. What?

This figure in red was asking me for help?

Had I misread everything?

The cold deepened. The figure shuddered. The skeletal fingers clicked together. The hood shifted, looked back over its right shoulder. Then back to me.

"Coming," its voice whispered. "They coming back for you."

I didn't like the sound of that.

"Lemme go." Even in the cold, my slur improved as I talked. "Then I'll help you."

It glanced back over its shoulder again. Then it released me. I fell back onto the carpet. The impact made my breath whoosh out of my lips, looking like steam in the dimness. I felt the skeletal hands flip me onto my stomach, then the bony fingers pushed mine out of the way. The ropes disappeared from my wrists. A moment later, my ankles were free.

My hands felt numb as I pushed myself to my knees. My hat lay a foot or so away. I grabbed it and stuffed it onto my head.

Standing took more effort. Muscles clenched and unclenched. It felt like they wanted to snap under the cold, but I finally gained my feet. Swaying but still standing, I looked at the figure in red.

"Can you get us outta here?" I asked.

A hand jerked up, pointing to the left. I turned. In the dimness, I could see the outline of a set of double doors.

I waved back at the figure. "C'mon."

My legs felt like stumps as I stumbled forward. I could almost feel my blood flowing sluggishly like thick syrup through my muscles. But every moment, it flowed a little faster, every moment, my muscles worked a little smoother. By the time I reached the door, I walked without limping.

But the figure behind me seemed to be having a harder time of it. Instead of gliding along, it lurched back and forth, gaining two steps before jerking back one. The feeling of menace rose up around it and I realized it wasn't coming from the red coated figure, but emanated around it.

Something else was controlling it, or trying to.

Was this what it wanted me to save it from?

I reached the door. The figure was still too far, still moving in a stuttering motion. The cold was deepening again, waves coming from the empty space between the chairs and counter. Whatever was coming, was showing up soon.

On a airplane they always said to put on your own mask before helping someone else.

But if I saved myself at this moment I might damn many others in the future.

I jumped back, grabbed the sleeve of the figure and yanked it after me.

Suddenly I felt like I was swimming in molasses. The air seemed to thicken, impeding my advance. The double doors, mere steps away, felt like miles. The cold deepened, laying heavy on my limbs. Even the rough fabric of the carpet seemed to scrape at the bottoms of my boots, trying to snag them as I shuffled forward.

"Go," the figure groaned.

I grit my teeth. "Yes, let's go."

I took a breath and focused before I made a final lunge. I could feel the web of cold and menace trying to snare me back. I focused on my own slim magic. I'd made a Chimney Jump once, something not even KJ had done. It was a magical leap up onto a roof, something Dad had perfected and he used it for homes that didn't have chimneys. He would land on the roof with the sleigh and magically "jump" into their homes to leave the presents, then "jump" back up to the roof. I'd done it by accident once when trying to escape an evil entity. I knew I could do it. But could I carry someone along with me? I don't even know if Dad could do that.

But I wasn't aiming for a roof, just to get out of the building.

I tightened my grip on the sleeve of the figure's red coat and *lunged.*

The cold shattered around me. A bone jarring impact hit my shoulder then gave. The door swung open before me. Fresh air rushed in. Snow puffed up as I leapt out.

The day seemed blinding bright after the darkness inside. My eyes watered. I blinked them to clear my vision. Grey sky, heavy with cloud, hung above me. White snow covered the ground and dotted the evergreens across the way.

"Noel!"

Venir's voice cut through the air. I turned to look right. The Elf ran forward then stuttered to a stop. His mouth dropped open.

"Behind you!"

I still had a grip on the figure's red coat. It swayed in the light, looking like it was going to fly away in the wind.

But beyond it, I could see the darkness thickening in the doorway, getting ready to pounce.

"Office now," I yelled at Venir and I *winked*.

CHAPTER

EIGHTEEN

I stumbled, hitting my left hip against the sharp edge of my desk. The sudden pain distracted me from the slicing pain in my temples. Beside me, at the corner of the desk, the figure in red sagged.

Finally I released its sleeve, peeling my fingers off as they felt like they'd been frozen to the fabric.

I pointed across the desk at the hard backed chair that sat in front of it.

"Sit," I said. "You and I are going to have a chat."

It moved with a slow lethargy around my desk before it sank down in the chair.

After the frigid cold, the heat in my office felt stifling. I let my coat slide off my shoulders. My legs shook a little as I took the few steps to the door and hung up my coat on the nail on the back. I dropped my hat on the side of my desk as I moved back around it to my leather chair. As I sat down, the figure reached a skeletal hand toward my hat.

Anger flared inside me. After everything that was going on, I knew it was irrational to be annoyed at this figure reaching for my hat but there it was. I grabbed the brim and yanked it toward myself.

"Don't touch," I said. "Talk. Who are you? What's going on? Why are you killing those people?"

The hood shook from side to side.

"Not me. Not killing."

"Then who?" I asked. "Who are you?"

"Boss."

Venir appeared in the doorway. He clenched his unlit cigar in his right hand, holding it up like a talisman against the figure in the chair.

Warmth flushed through me. It was silly at a time like this, but hearing Venir call me 'boss' again made me realize how much I missed having him around.

"Come in, Venir," I said. "This..." I waved at the figure. "Is just about to tell us who he is."

The figure shuddered. The red fabric of the coat shivered. The long, thin fingers gripped the edge of my desk.

"Yule Lads," it said. "I am part of them. One of them."

"See, I knew it," Venir said.

I held up my hand to stop the Elf's enthusiastic proclamations.

"You wanted revenge on what my father did?" I asked. "How he stopped you?"

The figure shook its head again. "No, I do not want this. None of us do. But we can't... help..."

It shuddered again, this time so hard, the hood slid back as the figure's head jerked back. The fabric slid away, revealing a man so pale his skin was greyish. Tiny ears pocked out from underneath greying hair. His cheeks were gaunt, exaggerating his angular nose even more than the first time I'd seen it.

In the hat shop.

Brendon.

I stared at him. He sagged back against the chair, his faded eyes were watery.

"You sold me this hat," I said.

Out of the corner of my eye, I could see Venir do a double take. Looking first at my hat then me, then back.

"To connect with you," he said. "So I could find you later."

I leaned forward, my forearms resting on my desk blotter. My hand was close to my silver letter opener, one of the magical desk supplies my mother had sent me. I had no idea what Brendon wanted but being within centimetres of the letter opener made me feel more prepared.

"You aren't making any sense," I said. "Starting doing so right now."

He wiped a thin hand across his mouth.

"It's difficult to talk," he said. "Difficult to say it outright."

Venir gave a loud sniff. "Smells like moth balls. Binding spell."

I glanced over at him. He nodded.

I looked back at Brendon. "That's why you sold me the hat. You couldn't come outright and talk to me. And you still can't, is that right?"

Brendon nodded. His neck was so thin I thought his head would snap off and roll toward me across my desk.

"Okay. Let's see how we can do this." I rubbed a hand over my chin and felt the full growth of my beard. After the day's events, I wasn't surprised that everything had grown back so fast. It was probably totally white too.

"You're one of the Yule Lads but you aren't doing this for revenge. Someone's bound you so you can't say outright. How am I doing so far?" I said.

Brendon nodded again. His thin lips twitched in a semblance of a smile.

"This someone, is it another one of the Yule Lads? One of your brothers?" I asked.

"No," Brendon said.

"Are all of the Yule Lads bound like you are?"

This time, the twitch was more of a grimace. He nodded.

"But all the menace I felt," I said. "Are you saying that wasn't directed at me?"

"Angry." Brendon spat out the word. He hunched over like he was going to heave.

I glanced over at Venir. He raised an eyebrow at me.

"Does this track?" I asked him. "Could something be that powerful to enslave them all?"

Venir shrugged. "If ya cast a strong enough spell, you can do almost anything. Gotta know the spell though and be able to control it. Aren't that many that know stuff like that."

"It would have to be really powerful magic to mess up the security tapes too," I said. "And affect Palle."

The Elf nodded.

I looked back at Brendon. He looked even paler, as if even hearing us talk about it pained him. He probably wouldn't be able to tell me and it probably would hurt him even more, but I had to ask.

"Who is doing this to you?"

His face twisted in pain. His nails dug into the edge of my desk. A moan tore from his mouth and ended in a gurgle. Red spittle bubbled between his lips as his jaw opened and closed as if he was trying to speak.

"Stop!" I said.

He gagged and took a ragged breath in.

So much for finding out the easy way.

I rubbed my forehead. My own temples pounded from the magical exertion I'd been doing. Even just sitting I could feel fatigue dragging at me, urging me to rest and recover. But there was no time.

Even though the call from Mallory had been faked, I had no illusion that he was a target, if only to get to me. He was prominent enough on his own to be a target even without the added bonus of his connection to me. The very least I could do would be to warn him.

But warn him about what? He wasn't able to see the Yule Boys, not without my influence and without having a seizure.

I grabbed the receiver and stabbed the buttons on my phone. I still had to warn him. No matter what.

The phone rang twice in my ear before Mallory's gruff voice answered.

"Where's Palle?" he asked.

Not even a hello. He'd recognized my number on the call display.

"I haven't found him," I lied.

"Sure you haven't," Mallory said. "I know he's your friend, Noel, but you have to bring him in. It'll get ugly if you don't."

"He didn't do it," I said. "But I didn't call about him. You need to listen to me. You have to be careful. I have reason to believe you're a target."

"What the hell are you talking about?" he said.

"It's something magical," I said. "All ten of the victims were killed by magic..."

"Ten!"

"I can't go over it all right now," I said. "If you could come to my office..."

"Stop, Noel. I want to believe you, to give you time, but it's not up to me. These are big cases and I can't just let our number one suspect skip out because we're friends. If you don't bring him in by tonight, I'm coming for him." He paused and I could hear him take a deep breath. "And for you for aiding and abetting."

"Stan!"

"I don't have a choice. Everybody's screaming for blood about this. The captain, the politicians, the public. People are terrified and it's worse this close to Christmas. Bring Palle in. It's the only thing you can do."

He hung up before I could reply.

I let the receiver drop from my fingers. It clattered as it hit the edges of the phone and settled into place.

Something he'd said fired something in my brain.

"What did he say?" Venir asked.

I held up a hand to stop Venir's questions. Something Mallory had said...

Every one screaming for blood. Especially at this time of year.

Christmas. It all had something to do with Christmas.

Of course it did. Using the Yule Lads as conduits. The timing heading into mid-December and causing a charity drive for children's toys to be disrupted. Everything pointed toward Christmas.

Whoever was doing this had a real bone to pick with the season.

I spun in my chair toward Venir.

"I need you to do some research, Venir," I said. "Find out who has a murderous resentment toward Christmas. The kicker is it has to be someone with enough magic to enslave the Yule Lads."

For the first time in weeks, a huge grin spread across the Elf's face. He pulled out a half smoked cigar out of his pocket and jammed it into the left side of his mouth. With his right hand, he gave me a salute.

"I'm on it, boss," he said. "Where are you goin'?"

I took a breath. "I'm heading to the police station." I glanced over at Brendon. "Mallory wants me to bring in Palle. I think I might take him someone else instead."

It was just after five by the time we reached the station but it was dark enough to look like midnight. Brendon trailed behind me, the hood up over his face as he bowed his head. He had his arms wrapped around his waist and he hunched over, shrinking his height.

But even as strange as he looked in the red coat with the matted fur trim, no one glanced at him. Whatever spell that bound him hid him from casual view.

Who could do that? And why? If I could answer one of those questions I could answer the other. But so far, I had no idea.

I pulled open the door to the precinct and stepped inside. Dry heat sucked the moisture from eyeballs, making them feel gritty. At the counter was a young officer with short blonde hair so pale I could almost see his scalp through it. I didn't recognize him from any of my other visits. Must be the weekend guy.

"I'm here to see Detective Mallory," I said. "He's expecting me."

The officer who looked like he might be older than twelve eyed me. "You're Kringle?"

I nodded.

He gestured at the metal detector to the right of the counter. I stepped through with no issue. I gestured at Brendon to follow.

"What are you waving at?" the officer asked.

As Brendon stepped through, the officer's gaze slid past him, unseeing.

That damn spell.

"Nothing," I said. "I'm going."

I began to head for Mallory's cubicle but was intercepted by another officer. She led me away from the cubicle farm and into a smaller office. It was empty except for a table and two chairs. Files and papers were spread across the table. Mallory sat facing the door as he tapped on a laptop computer. He grunted as I stepped inside.

"You bring him?" he asked, not even looking up.

"Not exactly," I said. "I brought someone else."

Mallory huffed out a breath, then sat back, finally looking up. He ran a hand over the short cropped greying brown hair on his head.

"Who?" he asked.

I looked over at Brendon who now stood beside me. He had pulled his hood back, revealing his gaunt profile.

"He's right here," I said. I reached out and touched Brendon's arm.

Mallory's gaze moved to my right. As soon as it reached Brendon, his eyes grew glassy and slid past.

Mallory frowned. "Where? Noel, is this one of your games?"

Brendon shook his head at me.

The spell. Even in the same room it hid Brendon from Mallory's gaze. This must have been how the Yule Lads could get so close to their victims. How could anyone be on guard against something they couldn't see?

And how was I going to convince Mallory when he wouldn't be able to see?

I pushed the brim of my hat back on my head.

Then grabbed the brim.

Would it work?

"Pay attention," I said to Mallory as I took off my hat.

He raised an eyebrow at me and tilted his head.

I turned to Brendon and set my hat on top of his head. It was a little too small, sitting on top like a child's hat and it sat too far forward, but I let it go.

I looked over at Mallory. He was frowning.

"What did you see?" I asked.

"I'm...not sure," he said.

"Try."

"You took off your hat and then..." His eyes narrowed as he concentrated. The lines on his forehead deepened. His breath came a little ragged.

Maybe this had been a bad idea. I didn't want him to have another seizure.

"Stan, stop," I said.

His head tilted. "Wait, is there a guy standing there?"

I held my breath.

Mallory blinked and shook his head. He pinched the bridge of his nose.

"Did you see him?" I asked.

"For a second, I saw... something," he said. "Christ, my head is pounding."

"It's a spell," I said. My words seemed to come in a rush, like I could protect him from the effects by explaining it. "It's a binding spell on the Yule Lads. Someone is making them do this and it's also hiding them from view, not only like this in the room but also on the security tapes."

Mallory's hand dropped to the table. "Noel, what the hell are you talking about?"

"The reason you could only sort of catch a glimpse of this man," I said, gesturing at Brendon. "It's a binding spell."

Mallory shook his head. "What man?"

"It's no use," Brendon said. "He can't see. He can't remember."

Burning coals, how was I going to convince Mallory when he couldn't remember what glimpse he had just seen?

I rubbed a hand over my face, feeling the scruff of my beard scratch my palm.

"Stan, I need you to trust me. There's a spell that's interfering with you. It won't let you see or remember what I'm trying to show you so you'll just have to trust me on this."

Mallory stood up and came out from behind the table. He stopped just in front of me. Under the yellowish fluorescent lights, his shirt still looked blinding white, the sleeves rolled up to his elbows. Only the slight wrinkling around the torso told me how long he'd been wearing the shirt. From this close up, I could also see the shadow of a beard growing on the contours of his face. If he'd been home and slept in the last two days, I would eat my new hat.

"I know you're trying to help, Noel," he said. "But none of what you said can be used in my case. I can't go to my superiors and say 'oh, it's a spell' and expect them to accept that. We need evidence, tangible reality. I can't wait any more. I would really prefer if you brought Palle in yourself. It would be better for him. But if you won't, we'll have to go after him. I can't wait any longer."

I glanced over at Brendon. He shook his head.

There was nothing else I could do here.

Nothing but protect Palle.

"Can you give me one more day?" I asked.

Mallory sighed. "You ask this every time."

"Just one."

"Noel..."

"Please? Until Monday night, I can stop this and you'll have the evidence you need."

His eyes narrowed. He lifted his hand and jabbed a finger into my shoulder.

"Monday until five o'clock. Any later and I'm coming for you as well as Palle. Got it?"

I nodded.

"Christ, I can't believe I'm doing this again."

I let a quick grin flash across my face. "You believe me, that's why."

"Get out," he said. "You've got less than twenty-four hours."

I hurried out before he could change his mind.

At least I'd gotten a one day reprieve for Palle and myself. Now I just had to solve these twelve murders, destroy the spell binding the Yule Lads, ensure Shirl got the right sleigh runners, and find a way to replace the toys for the Toy Stash.

Easy, right?

Sure. And my hair would stop turning white at Christmas.

NINETEEN

When we reached the street, a sprinkling of snow was drifting down from the sky. Steady traffic drove by in a hiss of damp asphalt. I breathed in the cold air, feeling it freeze the insides of my nostrils.

Almost cold enough to remind me of home.

Brendon didn't seem to notice the cold. He stopped in front of me as I jammed my hat back onto my head. It hid most of my white hair well. At least he knew hats.

"How do you propose to stop this in a day?" he asked.

I glanced around the street. Even on a Sunday, people were out on the street, hurrying along, loaded with bags from shopping. Of course it was almost mid-December. Who said all shopping was being done online?

"I'd like to talk to your brothers," I said. "Can you arrange it?"

Brendon shook his head. "They are still deep under the spell. I was the only one who was strong enough to break free."

Interesting. I was about to ask him about that when my cell phone rang. I pulled it out of my pocket.

"Hello?"

"Noel, I found something you should see," Palle said in my ear.

I cast a glance back at the precinct before I started walking away. I waved at Brendon to follow me. I knew no one in the station could hear our conversation but it still felt wrong to talk to Palle right in front of the main doors.

"I told you to call me later," I said.

"It is later," he said. "And this could not wait any longer. You really need to see this."

"All right," I said. "Tell me where you are and I'll meet you."

"It is a small forest called Sherwood Forest off Mount Pleasant. I will meet you at the bottom of the hill." He gave me the address. Before I could ask more questions, he hung up.

I folded my flip phone and stuffed it back into my coat pocket.

"You want to know how I'm going to stop this in one day," I said. "Follow and find out."

It was a great line, except when I turned to head for the

subway I almost bowled over a woman carrying two big bags.

"Watch out, you idiot," she said as I stumbled back. She shook her head as she hurried past.

Brendon pressed his thin lips together and followed me.

THE ENTRANCE TO SHERWOOD FOREST WAS DOWN A LONG CURVING road that was more like a long driveway without the benefit of streetlights. By the time we reached the bottom, it felt like midnight although it couldn't have been later than five in the evening.

The darkness was absolute. Traffic was a distant murmur, fading to silence. The air was crisp and cool, empty since the snow had stopped a little while ago. I breathed in the coolness, catching a hint of oak. But there was nothing else. Not even the sharp hint of pine.

And no one else.

Had it been a ruse?

A sound of snow crunching sounded behind me. I spun. The forest was a dark wall, the suggestion of trees a deep smudge against the blackness.

Then the smudge moved forward.

"Noel?"

I relaxed. "Palle."

He fiddled with something in front of him and a moment later a soft yellowish glow grew. An old fashioned lantern. He held it up, illuminating the area around us.

In the yellowish light, Palle's light green skin took on a deep green hue. His tusks glinted white. He had let go of the human disguise.

He smiled at me then the smile faded as he noticed Brendon.

"Who is that?" the troll asked.

"This is Brendon," I said. "He's a Yule Lad. They've been forced to do these killings by someone else. One of them cast the spell that framed you."

Palle frowned. His eyebrows drew in and his tusks looked even bigger as his lips pulled down. I managed not to take a step back although I did lean away. I'd never seen him frown before and I hoped never to again. It was terrifying.

"I'm sorry," Brendon said. "We are trapped."

"Maybe you can relate," I said quietly.

Palle's frown slowly faded. His gaze dropped from the Yule Lad. When I met Palle, he had been under the influence of a powerful spirit that had rode him across the barrier from the Magical Realms. It had forced him to do things he hadn't wanted to do.

"What did you have to show me?" I asked.

"Follow," he said. "It is better if you see yourself."

The troll turned away and headed for a dim path that cut through the darkness. As the soft light from the lantern moved with him, I saw the stark trunks of trees on either side of Palle.

We began to climb steadily upward on the snow-encrusted path. The lantern swung in Palle's hand, appearing and disappearing behind his large form. Even with its light, I could only see a few feet in front of us. The silence was thick and heavy. The chill deepened as we moved through the still forest.

At one point, the path branched and Palle led us to the right. The crunch of snow seemed almost hushed. The shadows seemed to get even deeper, darker. It felt like something was hiding in those shadows, ready to jump out at me.

I hunched my shoulders and tugged my hat a little farther down on my ears. If worst came to worst, I might be able to *wink* myself back to my office. But what about Brendon and Palle? If something attacked us, could I really leave them behind?

"I have been hiding here," Palle said. The sudden sound of his voice made me jump.

"The forest is easiest for me to avoid humans. I tried High Park but there are too many people there even though the park is much bigger than here. It is while I was here that I found what I want to show you."

He waved us down a narrow path to the left. The ground dipped sharply on the right. I noticed something sparkled below in the yellow light. A frozen creek bed.

Palle lifted the light higher. At the end of the creek, I saw a large metal square blocking the path of the water. Some kind of water regulator. That wasn't what Palle had brought me to see.

Just ahead of us, the snow had been swept away, leaving a bare patch of earth approximately ten feet in diameter. Marks had been scratched into the dirt and partially smudged out, but even partly obscured, I knew what those marks were and where my sudden fear had come from.

A spell. A powerful spell. Powerful enough to still leave a lingering effect even when it was completed.

I turned to speak to Brendon who was walking behind me.

He'd stopped at the turn off toward the creek.

Even in the dim light, I could see him shaking. The edges of his coat rippled like in a strong breeze. I started toward him. The sound of his teeth chattering together broke the stillness.

"Brendon," I said.

"She was... she was here." His words stammered out.

"Who was here?" I asked.

He shook his head. "I cannot... cannot..."

I moved closer, holding out my hands. "Take it easy. Just breathe. Tell me who it was." I jerked a thumb back in the direction of the dirt marks. "She's gone now. It's okay."

He shook his head again. I got close enough to see his eyes open wide and unblinking, the whites almost shining in the dark.

"Not gone. All of them.... Not gone."

What did that mean? I was about to ask him when I heard the crunch of footfalls on the snow. Several footfalls.

Coming from several different directions.

Maybe that sensation of being watched hadn't been just a figment of my imagination.

A moment later I could feel the menace pierce through the air.

Damn the halls.

I pushed past Brendon toward the entrance to the creek path. A stronger blast of menace.

They'd cut us off from the exit, and from what I could tell, every other way out. The frozen creek on one side, the rising hill covered with trees on the other.

I retreated back to Palle. The troll was holding the lantern high, casting the light as far as it would go. At the edges of the light, I saw shadows moving, but nothing stepped forward.

"Noel." Palle's voice was calm and quiet. "What do we do?"

My mouth felt parched. I licked my lips.

Good question. What could we do?

There were eleven Yule Lads surrounding us, enchanted by some unknown spell caster with some unknown spell. Questioning them about Christmas could halt them, but I had only managed it one at a time. Would I be able to fend off eleven enchanted Yule Lads at once?

I didn't want to risk it.

So what then? How could we fight them?

I glanced around. A few stray sticks and twigs littered the cleared ground. Snow piled around the edges of the empty space but held nothing of consequence.

I didn't think a snow ball fight would help us.

The cleared ground...

"Palle, the symbols. Redraw them!"

I lunged for one of the sticks as I heard the crunch of snow a few feet away. Someone was approaching from the hilled forest. From the sound of the footfalls, it was several someones.

Menace crawled up my neck. I clenched the stick and dropped to my knees. The ground was almost as hard as a rock. The stick snapped in my hand as I tried to trace the first line. I tossed away the broken end and reversed it.

Small scrapes. Like brushing at the ground, not like trying to draw a line.

The marks began to reform.

Palle set the lantern on the ground in the centre. He knelt across from me, scraping at the ground.

I finished one symbol. Moved to the right and worked on the next. And the next.

Cold thickened in the air, clutched at my muscles. But it wasn't the cold that made me shiver. The menace was like a wall, bearing down on us. In the dim light, I could see Palle shivering as well.

Where was Brendon?

I risked a glance back over my shoulder. I thought I saw him still standing at the entrance to the path leading to the creek. His head was bowed. As far as I could tell, he wasn't moving toward us, wasn't caught up in the drive of the spell, but he wasn't helping either.

It was probably all he could do to resist it.

I couldn't fault him for that.

I finished another symbol. Moved on.

Almost two thirds done. My hands were shaking from the residual power that was building underneath me. Even if we could finish redrawing the circle, would I be able to harness it to control the Yule Lads? Maybe it would just give them more energy to destroy us.

Next symbol.

Snow crunched to my right. I glanced over. A Yule Lad stood cloaked in a red coat, hood covering his face in shadow. The white fur trim was matted with dirt and blood. He lifted his thin hands, reaching toward me.

Menace blasted me, feeling like a physical wave, almost knocking me over. I put out my left hand to steady myself.

Smudged the symbol I'd been working on.

Oh clever.

But not enough.

I turned away from him, and focused on fixing the symbol. A few scrapes and done.

Next symbol.

Around us, the Yule Lads gathered, surrounding us. Even in the cold, I could feel myself sweating. My coat felt heavy on my shoulders, weighing my arms down. My hat itched on my head. I was sure that if my hair and beard weren't already white, they would have turned by now.

Good thing I wasn't bothering with the hair colour at the moment.

Next symbol.

The ground seemed to buckle under me. In front of me, Palle rocked back on his heels. He let out a startled roar. It echoed in the silence.

Good thing it was winter. In summer, he would have scared the hell out of the birds. Not to mention the hikers.

The Yule Lads took no notice. A final one stepped forward, closing the circle. The power of them made my skin crawl and itch at the same time. I kept wanting to look up at them, keep them in sight. But it was a distraction, even as the smell of ozone rose in the air.

I had to focus.

Next symbol. Last symbol!

I got halfway through when the howling started. A multitude of voices filled the air with the wailing, sounding like some horrific Christmas carol. Hands reached out toward us. Across from me, I spotted Palle growling, swiping at them. But they stayed just out of reach.

Why were they staying just out of reach?

We were in the circle. Even not quite complete, it served to protect us. And trap us.

If I couldn't gain control of magic in here, we'd never be able to leave.

The stick I was using snapped again, leaving me with a

splintered twig. Useless. I tossed it aside. I dug my fingers into the frozen dirt, scraping with my fingernails. Pain flared as one of my nails bent back.

Ignore it. Keep going.

Just a few more lines.

The howling chorus grew louder. Menace thickened in the air. Palle roared again.

"Hang on," I shouted. To him. To myself.

The final line.

I felt the power lock in like a jolt to my spine. It yanked me upright. I jumped to my feet, muscles protesting.

Around the circle, the Yule Lads stood, arms reaching out, hoods covering their faces although I imagined their mouths open wide, shrieking their horrid wail.

Then it stopped.

The Yule Lads vanished.

The regular cold rushed in, feeling like a wave of warmth. The feeling of menace faded. The power of the circle dissipated.

Was that it?

But...I hadn't done anything. I hadn't reversed the spell or changed it. I'd just redrawn the symbols to get ready for...

Oh no.

I'd screwed up.

Footsteps crunched on snow behind me. I turned.

Brendon hurried the last few steps to reach me. He gasped for breath like he'd run ten miles. His gaunt face was flushed. His eyes wide with fear.

"My brothers," he said. "She yanked them away. She's going after another."

"Where?" I said. "Can you tell where?"

His brow furled. Then he nodded.

"The Eaton Centre."

Burning coals, the Eaton Centre.

A shopping centre smack in the middle of the city.

Full of Christmas shoppers.

Burning coals!

CHAPTER

TWENTY

I had to get to the Eaton Centre. I turned to Palle.

"Find Venir, tell him to meet me at the mall."

"I should come with you," he said.

He stepped forward, towering over me like a dark mountain in the dim light from the lantern.

"I want you to stay out of this," I said. "It's too much risk for you to be out in public, Palle."

"But Noel..."

I held up a hand to stop him. "I appreciate you want to help. You can by finding Venir as fast as possible. Tell him to meet me at the mall. Then go back to the office and wait for me there. Can you do that?"

His wide shoulders sagged. He nodded.

I turned to Brendon. "Are you up for this?"

"Yes," he said. "It's the only way to free my brothers. They're caught in the web of the spell. I have to help them."

"Okay, then hang on."

I grabbed his arm and *winked*.

We landed in an alley across from the mall. Good thing as my legs almost gave out and I staggered to lean against the concrete wall.

Pain stabbed through my temples. I'd pushed too hard too often today for my meagre magic to deal with without rest. Now it was letting me know in no uncertain terms to cut it out.

I sucked in a lungful of exhaust-tinged air. The streetlights illuminated the alley, revealing the pristine blanket of snow behind me. In front, the sidewalk was well trampled with ragged mounds at the edge of the street. Cars rolled by in slow motion. Too much traffic to get up to speed.

Busier than I expected but then again, there were only a few weekends left before Christmas.

Finally the pain in my temples faded to a dull ache. I pushed away from the wall. Brendon stood in the centre of the alley, facing the mall across the street. He'd made no indication of noticing me as I recovered by the wall.

"Brendon? Are you all right?"

He started, head jerking around. He was so pale his skin was translucent.

"Yes...I..." He swallowed. "She is in there."

I nodded, then winced as a sharp pain stabbed my right temple.

"I'm sorry but I need your help to find her, to find your brothers," I said. "Can you help me?"

He shuddered then nodded. Pain etched deep lines around his mouth and across his forehead. He looked almost like I felt.

I stepped back to him and put a hand on his shoulder.

"We're going to stop this," I said. "You'll be free and so will your brothers."

His gaze, when he looked at me, was haunted. He nodded again without saying a word.

I released him. "I just wish you could tell me who 'she' is."

"Grinela." A gruff voice said from behind me.

I turned. Venir stood at the entrance to the alley. His parka was unzipped and his head was unadorned, like he'd grabbed his coat in a rush with no chance to put on a hat. His white hair curled around his pointed ears which rose high above his head. But even if he wasn't standing just inside an alley, out of direct sight of anyone on the street, no one else would notice his ears. His magic hid them from the view of normal people.

Except me. But I never said I was normal.

"Who is that?" I asked.

"She's the mother of the Yule Lads." Venir moved closed, his feet kicking up puffs of snow.

Beside me, Brendon seemed to sag deeper into his red coat.

"Why is your mother doing this?" I asked.

He opened his mouth and closed it again. Another shudder shook his body.

Whatever spell she'd cast, it was still keeping him silent. I would have to find the answers on my own.

I turned back to Venir.

"Okay, we know how she is," I said. "Do we know how to stop her?"

Venir shrugged. "She shouldn't even be doin' this. It don't make sense. Grinela causes mischief but it shouldn't be killin' like this."

"Well, it is," I said. "And we have to stop her." I pointed past him at the mall. "And we have to stop her now."

"Boss..."

"I'm going in there now," I said. "You can come and help me or wait here."

Venir puffed out a breath. "I'm comin' in."

"Then let's go."

We entered through one of the side doors into the centre of the mall. From here, I knew the mall went down two levels. Two more levels full of stores and shoppers.

On this level, the crowd didn't seem too large. A steady stream of people wandered past but there were large breaks between the groups of two or three.

The air was filled with the tapping of shoes on tile, the hum of voices, and the trill of music. Christmas carols, of course.

Decorations hung from the ceiling, long streamers of shimmering colour in red and green.

Almost directly ahead of us was an escalator going down. To the left, was a waist-high ledge. I moved toward it and looked down. The floor opened up to reveal the level below. The crowd was larger down there, bustling and shifting in lines that flowed through and around each other. I spotted more decorations, small trees at the sides of store doors. Brightly wrapped boxes piled in a pyramid shape.

And toward the middle of the mall, a pair of huge silver reindeer, shimmering in the light, standing beside a gigantic Christmas tree.

Would Grinela be able to resist that?

I headed for the escalator with Brendon and Venir bringing up the rear. As we descended one level, the sounds of the crowd grew louder, the voices murmuring, the footsteps, the rustle of bags both plastic and paper. I breathed in a cornucopia of smells, different perfumes warring with each other, a range of florals and musks, the yeasty scent of baked goods, the sweet pour of chocolate, buttery popcorn, and a hint of greasy fast food.

I let go of the rubber escalator railing as I reached the floor and stepped off. A woman in taupe coat crossed in front of me, pulling along a boy in a bright orange jacket. She cast a quick glance at me, then looked back. I tugged my hat down, touching the brim as if in a salute to her but using it as a way to hide my hair. She gave me a tired smile and then continued on.

This hat really had been a good idea.

Let's see what other good ideas I could come up with, and super fast because I had no real idea of how to stop Grinela. I just hoped something would occur to me.

I glanced back as Brendon and then Venir stepped off the escalator. Even under the bright, warm lights, Brendon looked pale and gaunt. He moved slowly and carefully, like a man afraid his bones would break.

"Can you tell where Grinela is?" I asked.

He raised his hand and pointed one skeletal finger down the centre of the mall. Toward the giant reindeer and the Christmas tree.

Exactly where the snow-covered peak of a fake cottage poked up through the crowd. Through the crowd of children with their parents.

Waiting to sit on Santa's lap.

Damn the halls.

"Kiddo, this don't look so good," Venir said.

I sighed. "You've mastered the obvious. Well, let's go."

He grabbed onto my sleeve, stopping me.

"How exactly are we gonna stop her?" Venir asked. "Ask her nicely?"

"I've noticed that every time the Yule Lads have attacked I've been able to stop them with images of Christmas," I said. "They have a connection to Christmas and that's the key.

When this all starts, I want you to get everyone out of here. That's your job."

The Elf shook his head. "But you still haven't said what you're gonna do."

"I'm going to give her the strongest connection to Christmas there is in this city. Me."

Before he could say anything, I pulled my sleeve out of his grip and headed into the crowd.

Soon I was surrounded by people, all moving forward like a quick-flowing stream. Brendon stayed by my side, gliding along. No one seemed to see him but no one got in his way. Every step forward, people parted as if somehow not wanting to get close.

I looked for Venir and caught a glimpse of his white curls bobbing back to the right. For a moment they stayed in view, then a large man in a dark blue, puffy jacket passed and I lost sight of the Elf.

He knew where we were going. I hoped he got there in time to help.

I swerved around a man pushing a stroller and then past a group of chattering teens. The fake cottage loomed large in front of me. Bright white walls and a peaked black roof with fake snow. More fake snow billowed around the bottom of the cottage, ending right at the back of a large, gold chair. A man in a Santa Claus outfit sat in the chair, hunching over the child on his lap. He was smiling merrily into the camera as the child, a young boy of perhaps three, looked up fearfully. He had his hand up to his mouth, fingers touching his lips, not sure if he wanted to smile or cry. Even from here, I could see the uncertainty on his face, the tremble in his lower lip. His gaze darted away from the woman dressed in the elf costume who manned the camera in front of the display.

And his gaze landed on me.

I gave him my best Santa smile.

The little boy's eyes widened in delight. His hand dropped down to his lap. A smile bloomed on his face as he relaxed completely.

The girl elf snapped the photo and then helped the little boy down from Santa's lap. As another woman, presumably the mother, took the boy's hand, he pointed toward me with the other. I could see his lips moving. Probably telling his mother that he saw the real Santa.

Then just behind the cottage, I spotted an old woman glaring out at me.

Grey hair cut short ended in wisps that accentuated her thin cheekbones. A slight overbite made her scowl deeper. Unlike the Yule Lads, she wore a long black coat with a high neck. Black fur trimmed the neck line and the wide sleeves, doing little to hide her clenched fists.

All the menace I had felt over the last few days seemed to concentrate and blast forth from her glare.

I wanted to turn away, curl up from her glare, but I couldn't. Not and let her continue killing. That's what she was here to do, kill someone else.

Kill this Santa.

On the left side of the cottage, a large sign proclaimed "Today only, Reg Harcastle as Santa Claus."

I'd heard of Harcastle. He was a popular theatre actor, appearing consistently at the renowned Stratford Festival. And Grinela was going to kill him, unless I could stop her.

The crowd lining up began to murmur and shift aside. Several children spontaneously burst into tears. Cries and wails rose into the air. Adults clutched the children to them. Creases and worry lines deepened on the parents' faces. Many people ducked their heads as they tried to push away through the crowd.

Then on the edges, I spotted the other Yule Lads.

They stood in a large circle, encompassing the Santa's cottage and the line of children, fanning out to take in a large crowd. People walked right past them, not glancing at the gaunt figures in red coats but giving them a wide berth.

A whimper sounded from behind me. I glanced back.

Brendon was almost bent over double, his arms wrapped over his head. I wanted to step back to comfort him but I couldn't move.

The menace seemed to creep over my skin like mounds of beetles. It let me know how foolish I was to think I could oppose her. I was nothing but a child, and a spare at that. Of no use at the North Pole and little use here. Bringing only mayhem and destruction to those around me. Why did I think this was all happening? It was because of me, my fault, my blame, my responsibility.

Because no Kringle was supposed to live in the day to day normal world.

I had broken the covenant. Broken the rules.

So now all the rules were broken.

I had let this happen.

I cringed under the assault. My legs shook and I dropped to my knees. Wailing sounded around me but it seemed muffled, distant. I bent forward to the floor. Grovelling. Asking for mercy. Forgiveness. I only wanted to live my life, to help people. I never meant anything bad to happen.

It was my fault.

Only one way to really repent.

My heart pounded in my chest. Sweat covered my body, dampened my hair under my hat. I could feel it running down the back of my neck, soaking my scarf, my shirt.

All I had to do was to look up and give myself over to her.

I could end this.

No one else would have to die. Only me.

It was the one thing I had to give.

Like a present.

But Christmas presents weren't given to ask for forgiveness. They were given to spread joy. Given to show love.

To share hope.

I lifted my head and through my bangs plastered to my forehead, I looked across at Grinela.

Her entire body was rigid with effort. Hands clenched in fists held to her chest. Arms squeezed tight against her torso. Her teeth clenched, her lips pulled back from them in a grimace. The veins in her forehead bulged. Even the roots of her hair were tense, making her hair stand on end.

Forcing her spell, her will on me.

Like all the Yule Lads.

And caught between us, the crowd of regular people wailed.

I could see them clutching each other, mouths wide open in silent screams, tears streaming down their cheeks. They pushed and shoved, trying to get away. Sorrow, pain, and fear etched in their faces.

They would be consumed if I didn't stop Grinela.

Maybe I wasn't supposed to be here, but neither was she.

And it was time for her to go.

I pressed my hands to the floor and pushed myself up to my feet. Out of the corner of my eye, I spotted something red. Brendon was curled into a fetal position on the floor, arms still wrapped over his head. Tears streamed down his face. He'd done everything he could to help me, even finding me a hat to hide my hair, yet I wasn't able to save him.

Stop.

I shook my head. No, she didn't get to worm her ugly thoughts into my head any more. I hadn't even begun to save him.

I turned back to Grinela.

And took off my hat.

I could feel the waves of my hair puff out. My beard felt full and bushy. I rivalled the Santa now cowering behind the gold chair. I'd brought joy to the boy who was about to cry.

I knew Christmas and I knew presents.

I focused on Grinela.

What's your favourite Christmas present?

Her mouth opened in a gasp. Her eyes widened as she recoiled.

I took a step forward.

What Christmas present gave you the most joy?

Her shoulders hunched. She clutched at the fur of her neck collar.

What Christmas present have you given that gave someone else joy?

She shrieked, her voice breaking through the wall of silence that surrounded me. I could hear the wails and cries of the people around me, still caught up in the mayhem of her spell.

I cleared my throat. "Santa needs a break. Please continue your shopping and return tomorrow."

The crowd turned away, searching for something. Heads turned this way and that, casting about for direction. I wanted to help them but even my momentary inattention had given Grinela a chance to catch her breath. Her hands had dropped from her throat. She sucked in lungfuls of air.

Preparing for her next attack.

I couldn't risk letting her complete it.

"C'mon, everyone, move it along, move it along." I heard a familiar gruff voice yelling out over top of the crowd.

Venir.

Already the crowd was turning toward him. I focused on Grinela.

Is this the kind of Christmas you wish for the Yule Lads?

She doubled over like I had punched her in the stomach.

I took several steps closer. The space between us emptied as the crowd drained away. Even the Santa had abandoned the gold chair. The entire display looked forlorn and empty.

Another step brought me within a dozen paces of Grinela. She glared up at me, fear and anger warring on her face. Her grey hair was matted with perspiration, sticking down to outline her skull.

I stopped in front of her.

"Why?" I asked.

She shook her head. Her teeth clenched. A growl sounded in her throat.

"You killed all those people, caused all that anxiety and attention around Christmas. Why?"

She howled at me.

"Why did you torment us?" said a voice behind me. I glanced over my shoulder. Brendon stood there, more colour in his face than even when I'd first met him. Around us, the rest of the Yule Lads had moved closer, throwing off their deep, red hoods, to reveal gaunt faces, flushed with anger and hurt.

Grinela began to shake. Her entire body quaked as those her joints had become undone from her bones. The smell of ozone filled the air, raising the hairs on the back of my neck.

A build up of powerful magic. An overdose.

"Watch out!" I yelled. I darted behind the cottage, landing at the foot of the gold chair.

Instead of running for it, the Yule Lads leapt forward, landing in a pile on Grinela's writhing form.

The spell snapped, sending a magical concussion through the entire floor. Light flickered and flared. Babies cried. Confused shouts filled the air.

My entire body felt like it had been stomped on. Muscles ground against bone as I pushed myself to my feet. About thirty feet away, I could Venir pick himself up off the floor, moving in the same old man way I felt.

And where Grinela was.

The Yule Lads parted, bent over and shuffling. In the middle of them was...nothing. Grinela was gone.

Gone at least from our realm.

I started to move toward the group when I felt a tug on my sleeve. I looked back. And then down.

A little girl with brown pig tails sprouting from either side of her head looked up at me with big, brown eyes.

"Santa, can I have a firetruck for Christmas? And my brother wants a build-a-blocks set."

I smiled down at her. "I'll see what I can do."

She beamed at me, then yelled over her shoulder. "See Brian, Santa's not scary. Stop bein' a baby."

Maybe Santa wasn't scary but Christmas almost had been.

CHAPTER
TWENTY-ONE

nce my hair was safely tucked under my hat, people stopped coming up to me as Santa, although the beard got a few looks. Within five minutes, the crowd had returned to normal, moving like a stream past the now-closed Santa's cottage. They gave a wide berth to the gathered Yule Lads but otherwise didn't seem to notice.

That was the thing about magical battles, if you weren't magical, you couldn't see them. And in the middle of a busy mall just before Christmas, that was a blessing.

"Where did you send Grinela?" I asked the group.

They looked at each other, then at Brendon.

"It wasn't Grinela," he said.

"What do you mean it wasn't Grinela," I said. "Who was it?"

"We don't know," one of the other Yule Lads said. "Under the spell, we believed it was she, but it was not. It was some creature from the Magical Realms, sent here to cause mischief."

The other Lads murmured their agreement.

"Twelve people are dead," I said. "That's a more than mischief."

Brendon glanced over at his brothers and then faced me. "We will investigate and I will tell you what we find."

At the back of the group, several of the Yule Lads faded. One by one they disappeared. Until all that was left was Brendon standing before me.

Before he could vanish, I grabbed his arm. "Brendon, check in with me regularly," I said. "This is the second time something has crossed over and caused deaths here."

Brendon frowned. "A second time?"

I nodded. "A while ago, when Palle crossed over. I think something else is going on, something big."

"I don't know what you mean," he said.

I shrugged and released him. "I don't know either. That's the problem. But it's strange that these magical problems are starting all of a sudden." My mouth went dry. "Maybe she was right."

"Whatever that creature said swas only to torment you," he said. "Do not take it to heart. That is how the spell gains strength, how it ensnared all of us. We believed her. But not now."

"Right," I said. "What about Palle? The security footage..."

"Will return to normal," Brendon said. "He did not kill so it will not show it."

Relief flowed through me, releasing a knot below my shoulder blades that I hadn't even realized was there.

"I must go," Brendon said. "My brothers await me."

"Thanks for your help," I said. "And the hat."

Brendon took my hand and shook it. "Thank you for saving us."

He let go. My palm still felt the warmth of his skin as he disappeared.

"Is she gone?" Venir stepped out from behind the Santa's cottage. He had his hands stuffed into the pockets of his khaki parka. His hair stuck out higher than normal.

"Yes," I said. "Let's get back to the office. I have to call Mallory."

MY OFFICE PHONE WAS ALREADY RINGING WHEN I *WINKED* BACK into my office chair. It creaked under me, listing just a little to the left. Another ring sent a sliver of pain from one temple through my brain to the other. Without even taking off my coat, I snatched up the receiver to stop the agony.

"Kringle," I said.

"Noel, something weird is going on," Mallory said in my ear.

I pulled my hat off and dropped it onto the side of my desk blotter. I rubbed my temple.

"What now?" I asked.

"The security tape from the Bengali Foundation," he said. "it's....it's different."

"What do you mean different?"

"There's some other guy on there." Mallory's voice got hushed, like he was whispering into the phone. "He gives the one security guard and Palle both a cup of coffee or something. A little while later, they both fall over asleep. Then he goes up the elevator and then comes back down with Troy Bengali's body. He stuffed it under the toy stash. Palle was asleep the whole time."

"Does that mean you don't want him to come in?" I asked.

"Well, he'll have to come in to fill out some paperwork," Mallory said. "Discharge of the charges. That kinda thing." He paused. "You don't think he'll sue or anything, do you?"

Palle suddenly filled the doorway to my office. Worry etched lines across the pale green skin of his forehead. His tusks turned downward in a frown.

"I'm sure a discharge of all charges will make Palle very happy," I said.

A smile bloomed across the troll's face. He clapped his hands together in delight.

"Great," Mallory said. "Bring him by tomorrow. Any time before noon. We have another suspect to find."

"Unfortunately I don't think you'll find him," I said. "But there won't be any more deaths because of them. I'm sure."

"Are you going to tell me what that means, Noel?"

"Later," I said. "Over a large glass of Gellers scotch."

"We can't just close down the investigation on your word," he said.

"I know," I said. "Just telling you you won't find anything."

He sighed. "I love my job."

The phone clicked in my ear. I set the receiver down.

"They are dropping the charges?" Palle asked. "You are sure?"

I stood up and slipped my coat off my shoulders. "We'll go down and fill out some paperwork tomorrow and it's all over."

"Noel, thank you! You've saved me again."

A moment later I was squished by a troll hug. My breath whooshed out of me. The intense pressure made it impossible to draw in more air. Trapped at my sides, I could only flail my hands. My face was squished against Palle's chest. I turned my head to the right, enough to free my jaw.

"Palle...can't breathe."

"Thank you so much, Noel," the troll said. "I cannot tell you how much I appreciate..."

"Can't breathe!"

"Oh."

He released me so fast I staggered, bumping against the wall as I grabbed for the desk. Fortunately my office was so small it would almost be impossible for me to fall right over.

I drew in a lungful of air. The stars that had started flickering in my vision faded. Another breath and I could stand upright without wavering.

"Sorry, Noel," Palle said.

I returned to my chair and settled down. "That's quite all right, Palle. You've had some very stressful days. Why don't you go home and relax? Tomorrow we'll head down to the precinct and take care of that discharge. Okay?"

The grin on Palle's face widened, making his tusks even more prominent.

"Yes, Noel. See you tomorrow."

He left. I sagged back against my chair and closed my eyes. Over, it was over. But I still had to wonder if there was some truth in what the fake Grinela had said. Were these things happening because I had come down from the North Pole? Had I made a huge mistake coming to Toronto? Had I unwittingly unleashed these magical catastrophes?

These were questions I was going to have to ponder in more detail. Maybe when I hadn't been battered in a fight.

I could almost feel the lure of my bed in my apartment tugging at me. But I couldn't go home quite yet.

I opened my eyes. Still at least one more thing to deal with.

I turned on my laptop and checked my email. At the top was a message from Shirl. She'd found the sleigh runners and they would be available by Wednesday. I forwarded her message to KJ with a note that he needed to pay her immediately with an additional bonus as a finders fee. I cc'd Shirl so she'd see it and cc'd the North Pole accounting office so they would know to follow up on payment. KJ wouldn't be able to delay or try to cut her out of her due.

That finished, I turned the laptop off and closed the lid. Now I just had to figure out a way to replace all the toys in the Toy Stash. I supposed if worst came to worst, I could buy them, although I didn't think I had enough money to replace all of them. Not even a quarter of them.

What else could I do? I sighed. I suppose it was better than nothing.

"Noel?"

Venir stood just beyond the doorway to my office. He had his hands stuffed into the pockets of his parka. His hair was still a wild mess around his head, almost but not quite covering the tips of his pointed ears.

I waved him in. He stepped into my office with a care he'd never shown before. He closed the door behind him, something I usually never did. I gestured at the hard-backed chair in front of my desk. He glanced at it and paused as if considering it, then he climbed up onto it. He sat with his feet dangling over the edge.

"Thanks for your help," I said.

He shrugged under the parka. "I didn't do much."

"You helped save people, get them out of the way. That's a lot."

He glanced down. "You always been good to me, kid. Even if I don't deserve it."

"Why don't you deserve it?" I rested my forearms on my desk blotter, trying to look casual.

"With all I done," he said.

"Venir, you don't have to tell me if you don't want to," I said. "Your past is the past. It doesn't have any bearing here."

"It does," he said. "It's who I am." He wiped a hand over his brow. "Too damn hot in here."

"Your coat," I said.

"Oh yeah." He shrugged out of the parka, revealing a brown, cable-knit sweater. He pushed the sleeves up to his elbows, then gripped his knees with both hands.

"I been wantin' to tell you," he said. "But I don't know how."

I didn't say anything, just waited. It seemed the best way to just give him the space to talk if he wanted.

"I were a supervisor at the North Pole, third shift. Lots of finishing and testing. Cream o' the crop. Very prestigious among the Elves. Lots of 'em wanted on the third shift so I had my pick of the crew. I tried to be fair and rotate on a regular basis, give everyone a chance for the glory. But some didn't like bein' rotated out. They figured they was due to be on the third shift for the entire time cuz they had seniority."

His hands gripping his knees tightened until his knuckles whitened. I stayed silent.

"Several of 'em got together and made a plan. Went to bosses and to KJ, saying rotating the shift was bad for quality assurance. See, rotating the shift was my idea, to give all the Elves the experience. It was new and very popular with 'em, even if management weren't so sure. After they tattled, KJ and the bosses visited the floor, checked some of the toys."

He stopped, squeezing his lips tight together. I waited, breathing slowly to stop myself from asking.

After a few moments, he started again.

"The toys were all broken, not working. They'd been sabotaged by these few Elves. KJ and the bosses were furious and rightly so. Blamed me and my innovation. Changed it back to the senior Elves took over the third shift like before. I got demoted back to the stables. Weren't even allow to make nothin'."

"Did you tell anyone that the one group had sabotaged everything?" I asked.

He shook his head. "No point. Nobody'd believe me. Yer brother sure wouldn't."

No, KJ wouldn't. That sounded exactly like him. When he made up his mind about something, he became practically entrenched in it.

"So when I heard that rumour from an old friend about someone killin' Santa, I decided to come down here and tell you. Nobody up there woulda listened to me."

I nodded, remembering the note I'd received and our first meeting by the fountain at Centre Island.

"Thanks for telling me, Venir," I said. "I'll be honest. I'm glad it happened."

He looked up, his brow draw in and his mouth tight.

"If it hadn't, I wouldn't have such a valuable asset on my team."

A blush reddened his cheeks and spread up to his hair line. He blinked rapidly as his eyes became watery.

"Thanks, kiddo." His voice sounded a little gruffer than usual.

I gave him a tired smile. "How about we get out of here and start fresh tomorrow?" I started to push myself up from my chair.

"Um, there is just one more thing," he said.

I stopped halfway up, hands resting on my desk blotter. "Oh?"

"I still got some friends up north, mostly the younger ones. I know you said you'd figure it out but…"

He slid off the chair, leaving his parka in a pile on the seat. He grabbed the door knob in both hands and twisted. Then he pulled the door open.

A trickle of toys fell in from the waiting room. Beyond the door frame, I could see them piled almost to the ceiling. Dolls and cars and trucks and spaceships and crayons.

It still wasn't quite enough to replace everything from the Toy Stash, but it was a fantastic start.

"Thank you, Venir," I said. "I should be able to buy enough to cover the rest of them."

"Oh this is just the first shipment," he said. "The other one'll be delivered to the Bengali Foundation tomorrow night." He grinned. "After the third shift."

"Are you sure there's enough overage to cover all of these toys?" I asked.

His grin widened. "Oh yeah, my friends are workin' triple time."

I smiled. "To make that third shift work harder."

He chuckled. "So hard there's no time for chattin' or muckin' about and they don't get their breaks. And the quality assessors are being real picky with such a heavy load."

I laughed and he joined in. At least I would be able to fulfill Troy Bengali's final Toy Stash and with a record number. It wouldn't bring him back but it would make a nice tribute.

"Thanks again, Venir," I said.

"Thank you, kid," he said. He coughed, and his voice came out gruff and choked. "You gave a broken Elf a new purpose."

I smiled. "You're welcome. But there is one other thing you could do before we head home."

He swallowed. "What's that?"

I lifted up a white curl from the side of my head.

"Help me colour this hair brown again?"

He grinned. "It's a losin' battle, kid, at least until the twenty-fifth."

I sighed. He was right and I did have the hat to cover it. Mostly. But burnt coals, I would never say die.

"Please?" I asked.

He rolled his eyes and gave an elaborate sigh. "Okay fine.

As long as we can cut it shorter."

"I shaved it all off earlier," I said as I stepped out from behind my desk.

"When?"

"Ah, that might have been this morning?"

"You damned Kringles." He shook his head. "C'mon, let's get it done."

He stomped through the waiting room, past the pile of toys, toward my bathroom.

"You still got the hair colour I bought?" he called back.

"It should all be in there," I said.

"Then let's do it already," he said.

I gave one last look to the pile of toys filling my waiting room. Even my sagging, brown leather couch was covered.

"Kringle," he yelled.

"Coming," I said. I picked up a teddy bear that had fallen to the floor and placed it gently in the middle of the pile.

Maybe I never would be Santa Claus but this was the next best thing.

"Kringle!"

"All right," I yelled back.

"Move it or yer doin' it by yourself."

"I won't be able to by myself," I said.

He poked his head out the bathroom door. "Then get a move on."

He had an annoyed, indignant look on his face but I could see the twinkle in his eye.

You could take the Elf out of the North Pole...

I stepped into the bathroom and crouched so he could reach my head.

"Let's cover this so I look less like Santa, at least for a few days," I said.

"And when it stops workin'?" he said.

"Then I'll wear that hat."

"Sounds like a plan," he said, and started snipping.

JOIN MY NEWSLETTER!

If you enjoyed this story, please consider taking a moment to review it or to recommend it to your friends. Reviews help other readers decide if a book is for them.

Sign up for my New Releases mailing list and get a free copy of the *Rebecca M. Senese Sampler*, featuring stories of science fiction, urban fantasy, mystery and horror. Enjoy them all!

Click here to get started: https://rebeccasenese.com/newsletter/

Santa's son is on the case
Enjoy more Noel Kringle with The Noel Kringle Chronicles!

REBECCA M. SENESE
Santa Claus:
PRIVATE DETECTIVE
THE NOEL KRINGLE CHRONICLES

REBECCA M. SENESE
SANTA MUST DIE!
THE NOEL KRINGLE CHRONICLES

REBECCA M. SENESE
THE CLAUS CONNECTION
THE NOEL KRINGLE CHRONICLES

REBECCA M. SENESE
BABY, IT'S DEADLY OUTSIDE
THE NOEL KRINGLE CHRONICLES

REBECCA M. SENESE
DO YOU FEAR WHAT I FEAR
THE NOEL KRINGLE CHRONICLES

REBECCA M. SENESE
THE MAN WHO WOULD BE SANTA
THE NOEL KRINGLE CHRONICLES

ACKNOWLEDGMENTS

Special Thanks to all of the generous folks who sponsored me for the 2017 Muskoka Novel Marathon, benefiting the YMCA Literacy Services of Huntsville. I wrote the first 88 pages of this novel at the marathon and couldn't have done it without the generous support of these fine people:

Chris Ainsworth, Paul Clinton, David Shtogryn, Louise Clare, Deb McGarvey, Jason Hildebrandt, Lillian Parkinson, MB, Andrea Strom, Matthew Andaloro, Gloria & Brian Williams, Teen Huang, Gary Grisdale, Maura Dales, Donald Simmons, Greg Hislop, Hector Turner, Lily Lee, Iman Hamed, Jenny Chiu, Betty Wong, Julie Florio, Sheri Wilkinson, Bob Clinton, Mandy Slater, Brenda Clark, Jennifer Kerr, Arnold Pereira, Carl Chalupa, Alison Meeks, Gaetano Gigliotti, Carolyn Sitler, "Titanium" Tim Blahout, Ross Darlington, Nadia Judges, Russell Martin, Al Chiasson, and Laureen Moran.

About the Author

Based in Toronto, Canada, I write horror, science fiction and mystery/crime, often all at once in the same story. I am the author of the contemporary fantasy series, the *Noel Kringle Chronicles* featuring the son of Santa Claus working as a private detective in Toronto. Garnering an Honorable Mention in *"The Year's Best Science Fiction"* and nominated for numerous Aurora Awards, my work has appeared in *Home for the Howlidays, Bitter Mountain Moonlight: A Cave Creek Anthology, Promise in the Gold: A Cave Creek Anthology, Unmasked: Tales of Risk and Revelation, Obsessions: An Anthology of Original Stories, Fiction River: Visions of the Apocalypse, Fiction River: Sparks, Fiction River: Recycled Pulp, Tesseracts 16: Parnassus Unbound, Ride the Moon, Tesseracts 15: A Case of Quite Curious Tales, TransVersions, Deadbolt Magazine, On Spec, The Vampire's Crypt, Storyteller, Reflection's Edge, Future Syndicate* and *Into the Darkness*, amongst others.

Find me online:
www.RebeccaSenese.com

www.NoelKringleChronicles.com
www.RebeccaSeneseBooks.com

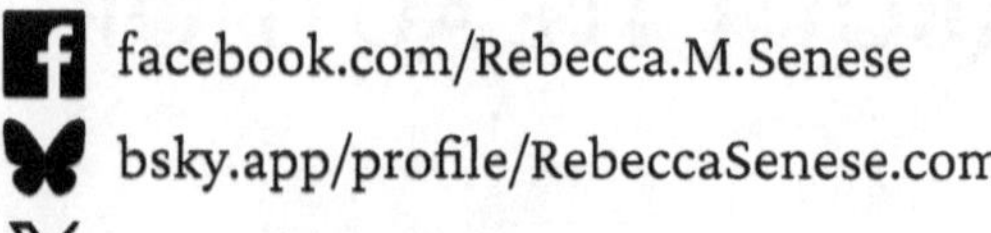

facebook.com/Rebecca.M.Senese

bsky.app/profile/RebeccaSenese.com

x.com/RebeccaSenese

bookbub.com/authors/rebecca-m-senese

instagram.com/rebeccamsenese

goodreads.com/rebecca_senese

wandering.shop/@rebeccasenese